EDITORS
Susan Burmeister-Brown   Linda B. Swanson-Davies

CONSULTING EDITORS
Kimberly Bennett   Allyson Bourke
J. Jackson Reynolds   Roz Wais
Chanda Wakefield

COPY EDITOR
Scott Stuart Allie

PROOFREADER
Rachel Penn

TYPESETTING & LAYOUT
Paul Morris

ADMINISTRATIVE ASSISTANT
Kaylin Elaine Dodge

COVER ARTIST
Jane Zwinger

STORY ILLUSTRATOR
Jon Leon

PUBLISHED QUARTERLY
in spring, summer, fall, and winter by **Glimmer Train Press, Inc.**
710 SW Madison Street, Suite 504, Portland, Oregon 97205-2900
Telephone: 503/221-0836   Facsimile: 503/221-0837
www.glimmertrain.com

PRINTED IN U.S.A.
Indexed in *The American Humanities Index.*

Glimmer Train (ISSN #1055-7520), registered in U.S. Patent and Trademark Office, is published quarterly, $32 per year in the U.S., by Glimmer Train Press, Inc., Suite 504, 710 SW Madison, Portland, OR 97205. Periodicals postage paid at Portland, OR, and additional mailing offices. POSTMASTER: Send address changes to Glimmer Train Press, Inc., Suite 504, 710 SW Madison, Portland, OR 97205.

ISSN # 1055-7520, **ISBN # 1-880966-39-5**, CPDA BIPAD # 79021

DISTRIBUTION: Bookstores can purchase *Glimmer Train Stories* through these distributors:
Ingram Periodicals, 1226 Heil Quaker Blvd., LaVergne, TN 37086
IPD, 674 Via de la Valle, #204, Solana Beach, CA 92075
Peribo PTY Ltd., 58 Beaumont Rd., Mt. Kuring-Gai, NSW 2080, AUSTRALIA
Ubiquity, 607 Degraw St., Brooklyn, NY 11217
SUBSCRIPTION SVCS: EBSCO, Faxon, Readmore, Turner Subscriptions, Blackwell's UK

Subscription rates: Order online (www.glimmertrain.com)
or by mail—one year, $32 within the U.S. (Visa/MC/check).
Airmail to Canada, $43; outside North America, $54.
Payable by Visa/MC or check for U.S. dollars drawn on a U.S. bank.

Attention established and emerging short-story writers: We pay $500 for first publication and onetime anthology rights. **Visit our website for guidelines on submitting your work online.**

Glimmer Train Press also offers **Writers Ask**—*nuts, bolts, and informed perspectives— a quarterly newsletter for the committed writer. One year, four issues, $20 within the U.S. ($26 beyond the U.S.), Visa, MC, or check to Glimmer Train Press, Inc., or order online at www.glimmertrain.com.*

Dedication

As this fortieth issue goes to press, we are taking
some time to review the names on page 183. Each
name included there has a history attached to it,
from the moment we first recognized a manuscript
as one we simply could not pass up (an indescribable
joy), to a tender note attached to a childhood photo
that the author's mother had sent in for the profile
page, This is my boy taken on his fifth birthday.

It is mentally and emotionally deeply satisfying work.
We could not do it without the good help of those
whose names appear on the page facing this one
you are now reading, nor without the support
of our subscribers. We are thankful to you all.

And one last heartfelt thank you on this occasion to
our husbands and children, who not only good-
naturedly accept that our cars and homes will always
be teeming with some of the 40,000 manuscripts
we receive each year, but who also share our great
pleasure as each new issue is sent off to press,
and again a few weeks later when the first bound
copies come to us looking maybe slightly more
beautiful than we had imagined they possibly could.

Susan & Linda

$\mathscr{C}$ONTENTS

CONTENTS

Carol Roh-Spaulding

Just the way I like it—a spacious and sturdy desk
between me and the rest of the world!
In August of 1999, my son was exactly the age I am
in this photograph—one month shy of age two.
Our resemblance (minus the hair) is uncanny.

Carol Roh-Spaulding was born in Oakland, California, in 1962, and now lives in the Midwest with her son, Jonah. She is assistant professor of English at Drake University, where she teaches fiction writing and American ethnic literature. Her fiction and poetry have appeared in several journals, including *Ploughshares*, *Amerasia*, the *Beloit Fiction Journal*, and the *Pushcart Annual XVI*, and have been anthologized in several collections, including *Writing Fiction*, *Love Stories for the Rest of Us*, *Other Sides of Silence: New Fiction from Ploughshares*, and *Asian American Literature*. Her awards include the Heathcote Award from the National Society of Arts and Letters, and a Cohen Award from *Ploughshares* for the best story of the year. She is completing a thematic collection of short stories and is compiling an edited collection of literary scholarship on mixed-race in Asian American literature.

CAROL ROH-SPAULDING
White Fate

*N*ot that he would ever allow himself to show it, and not that it would have made much difference in her upbringing if he had shown it, but the youngest of his three girls, Gracie, was Mr. Song's favorite. All morning, he had been dialing Gracie's number from the barbershop. She was probably out shopping with her sister Sonya and her baby niece, but he cleared his throat and kept practicing the right tone of hello, in case she answered. It had been a whole month since she had breezed into the front door with her new hairstyle, her new smile, and then stormed out again before she'd been home an hour, slamming the door shut behind her. A whole month since the argument with her mother, and still not so much as a telephone call.

Song kept himself occupied between attempts to reach her on the phone. He swept up the black clippings from young Jasper Woo's haircut, and the steel-colored clippings of Jasper's father, Elmer Woo. "Still have that daughter to marry off, Song?" Old Woo always asked when he came in. "What did you tell me she was studying? Was it science, hmm? Or mathematics?" Song just faked a contented hum by way of response. And then Old Woo had added—bit off the word and threw it at him—"Your daughter is *ambitious*, Mr. Song."

Glimmer Train Stories, Issue 40, Fall 2001
©*2001 Carol Roh-Spaulding*

Song never gave Old Woo the satisfaction of responding to his suggestion that his daughter was too studious, too masculine to make a good wife. What did Woo know about having daughters? Song put the linens in the hamper, rinsed the combs in the antiseptic, and went back to the telephone to try again. *Gracie,* he practiced. *Your mother and I would like the chance to talk with you about this... gentleman.*

That young Jasper Woo had turned out all right so far, thought Song. He was a former schoolmate of Gracie's who had taken over Woo's Bakery just like everyone had expected he would, married the tall, quiet Chinese girl his parents had found for him, and settled down and had two children. The boy was good to the old man, brought the grandchildren around on Sundays, helped his mother on with her coat. No denying it, Old Woo had done a good job with his boy. Every morning and every evening, if it wasn't raining and the fog wasn't too thick, Old Woo strolled around Merritt Lake, his hands clasped behind his back, his lips pursed contentedly like a Buddha's, with a look that said, "My work in life is finally done."

He set the receiver back down and stared at the month of September on the calendar from Chong's Fish Market. A Chinese beauty in a fierce shade of yellow smiled knowingly from behind an embroidered parasol. It was not without some satisfaction that Song polished the chrome in his barber chair and oiled the seat leather, and wiped the glass door with the bell that jangled when someone entered, and the windows, until they were completely free of streaks. He liked order. He liked order's sameness. But this morning he felt a restlessness that belied the tidy appearance of his shop.

Why hadn't either of his elder daughters been interested in a boy like Jasper Woo? And why hadn't Gracie? Instead, the older girls had eloped in the very same week, one of them with a Negro and the other with a Chinese who crooned the night away at the Oriental clubs in San Francisco. At first it appeared his wife, Jungmi, would never recover from her anger and shock, but along came a grandson, plump as a steamed pork bun; and then a black-eyed granddaughter with skin the color of richly steeped tea. They weren't the Korean babies Jungmi had wanted her daughters to have, but at least everyone was communicating again.

Although he did not express this opinion to anyone, least of all to Jungmi, Song could not entirely blame his daughters for their disobedience, caught as they had been between the failure of an expensive matchmaker to find a suitable Korean boy for either of them, and the American custom of letting passion decide your fate. In Korea, the family would have been disgraced beyond repair at the loss of two daughters to an uncertain future. Gracie would have had no chance of marriage after that. But this was not Korea, and far from being out of the question, Gracie's marriage now seemed imminent.

Five years earlier when she had been just out of high school, she had come in and sat before him on the footrest in front of his chair. Her deep blue dress was sprinkled with white dots of various sizes, and her shoulders shone clean, like little moons. "I wanted to ask you first," she began. "If there's no chance you'll say yes, then there's no use bringing it up with Ma." She cleared her throat. "I want to … I'm going to college."

Song answered simply, "You're a girl, Gracie."

She bit her lip and looked towards the back laundry, as though understanding this was more her mother's reply than his own. "I'm not asking for your permission, Daddy, I'm asking for your help." Her chin trembled with determination. In the end, he had given his consent despite Jungmi's protests, convincing her that it would be better to send Gracie to college themselves than have it be known that yet another daughter had disobeyed their wishes. Privately, Song hoped that Gracie's education would buy them all some time before the question of marriage was revisited in the Song household. Now his straight-backed, clear-eyed daughter was only one semester away from her university degree.

Song's gaze wandered the street outside the barbershop as he listened to the line ring. It was a bright and breezy morning, the kind of morning when his heart always lifted with a little chirp of abandon, filling him with the brisk promise that some of the things he had always longed for could still be his. If he wanted to, for instance, he could lock up the shop, cross the street to the laundry, fetch his wife, who would be pinning shirts about now, and take her out on the lake in one of those little green rowboats. He smiled to himself. The truth was he wasn't that kind of man.

He heard ringing, then a click. "Hello?"

Song's heart pounded. "Gracie?"

It was his daughter, Sonya. Gracie was studying at the library, she told him. She missed them both and would visit as soon as she finished her last exam. A moment of resentment lit Song's insides. It was Jungmi who had announced that she would never step foot into Sonya's place while they housed that rebellious college daughter of hers, Jungmi who was keeping everybody apart.

During the first couple of years, Gracie had come home on weekends to fold laundry, clean out the sinks, and sweep the barbershop. Slowly it became every other weekend. Even by the time Gracie was a junior it was difficult to adjust to her absence from home, because the Gracie that visited every other weekend kept changing in subtle ways. One day there was something more confident in the way she held her shoulders, in the lift of her chin. Slim-fitting pants and pearl-buttoned sweaters replaced her handmade dresses and neatly starched collars. Then the phone was always for her, and she answered with a special hello that Song had never heard her use with anyone else, a private hello, as though other people listening were not even present.

And then a month ago a dozen white roses had been delivered to their door. Gracie had breezed in to help in the laundry, and when she kissed her father hello, a sweet scent broke softly open all around him. She stood in the kitchen with her mother, wrapping Sunday dinner's *mahn-doo* dumplings. At her lips was a small, secret smile.

"This *miguk* not realize white color means death for Oriental people!" Jungmi complained to Gracie in dangerously pitched English. She spoke English when she wanted to get Song's attention. "What man do this sending white roses?"

"Of course I want you to meet him, Ma. His name is Wayne. Wayne doesn't care what white means to Oriental people."

"What, you ashamed being Oriental girl?" she shot back. "Let me tell you something," and she poked Gracie in the arm like she was testing the ripeness of a melon. "You. Oriental. Girl," she said. "You Chinese. You Japanese. You *Siamese* to this boy! Why he want to marry Oriental girl?"

"Ma!"

"Why he don't like American girl?"

"Stop it, Ma."

Song's teeth came together. The women's voices began again, low, but churning underneath, like the Beethoven pieces Gracie played on the piano, which began solemnly and then crescendoed with little warning into a violent outburst. Song braced himself behind the *Oakland Tribune*, but in place of shouting came a sound he had not expected. No broken glass, no spilled water, no tears. Only the thwack of twelve roses smacked against the wall by their stems, then a woman's high gasp, and white petals fluttering.

Gracie shot out of the kitchen, her handbag over one arm,

a fist of bedraggled stems in the other. She slammed the door so hard that the old cuckoo clock donated to the Songs in their first year in Oakland by the Presbyterian Women's Relief Society sounded above the piano. "Kook," it yodeled, half in, half out of its little door.

Silence limped through the house for a few weary minutes. Finally, his wife came out, whipping at the back of his chair with her feather duster. "I hope you're happy, my husband. Ha! Sending her off to college!"

Song sat back down on the sofa, crossed his legs, and picked up his newspaper. "A white wedding," he said as the feather duster went off to attack the coat tree in the hall. "That's what they call it in America." What else would you call it if your daughter was planning to marry a white man?

Now Song hung up the telephone and sat down with a sigh at the little corner table in the shop where he counted receipts or wrote his Sunday-school lessons between customers. How quickly it seemed his children had assumed this life of sky-scrapers, and cars with houses built right into them, and burgers with thick slabs of cheese that shined. It was as though their fate had simply greeted them at the door. He had been just eighteen when he first sailed out of Pusan Harbor only months before the long years of the occupation. If he was going to speak a new language, let it be English, he'd told himself, not Japanese. It wasn't until he was nearly forty, and already exhausted, that he had earned enough to bring his wife back to start a family.

As a girl, Gracie had worn a little blue pea coat that had been her sister's. It was an old but sturdy little coat, and so becoming on her. They had had a tradition, Song and his youngest daughter. Every Sunday afternoon after dinner at the Korean Methodist Church she would enter the shop and head straight to the cash register and ping it open. Out popped the drawer, and she would reach her fingers in and pull out two dimes for a ticket each to go to the Lux Theater. This was his cue to take off his white karate-style barber's jacket, hang it on its hook, and put on his coat and hat. Then the two stepped down the street, paid their dime each, and went in to watch the news of the war, and the cartoons, and then Bette Davis or Frank Sinatra or Ingrid Bergman or Spencer Tracy, all the greats. He would slip his hand into his pocket and pull out a piece of taffy or a licorice drop, and Gracie would take each candy one by one as though she had been brought to earth to relish a piece of candy perfectly and completely. She was so sure of her toffee, her caramel, her peppermint, sitting there by his side in that strangely lit dark with the hushed and solemn carpet, and the brocade-covered walls, so sure that she never even had to look at him or at his proffered hand to know that candy was coming. And if the candy did run out when the picture wasn't over, she would eventually reach over and hold his hand and sometimes lean her head on his shoulder. Once or twice this way she even fell asleep.

Song opened his eyes, realizing that he had been dozing. He looked over the top of his glasses at the figure of a very large man filling up the doorway. The man had a good smile—a proper kind of smile—and improbably red hair. His hand-shake was so vigorous you had to admire his energy. "I'm Wayne Teller," he announced. Song knew who he was. He freed his hand from Wayne Teller's enthusiastic grasp, and because he did not know what next to do, he gestured toward one of the barber chairs. "Please," he summoned him, hoping to sound commanding.

As soon as the man had settled into the chair, Song whisked an apron around his neck and pumped the chair down with his foot. He had a reputation with some of the sailors for giving a good haircut, cheap, so he knew Caucasian hair. This Caucasian had freckles even on his ears, and smelled of a tangy aftershave. He seemed to squint from sheer happiness while Song clipped above his ears, whacked away at the top. Song felt a little like a fly buzzing around an elephant. He straightened himself and pulled his own broad shoulders back. "Soooo. You work?" Song inquired, conversationally.

Wayne's eyes slid in the direction of the clippers. He cleared his throat. "I'm studying city planning, sir."

"Yes?" Song replied. He combed. He clipped. He shaved the back of the man's neck and whisked away the stray hairs with his feather brush.

"Sir?"

"Yes?"

His hand rose when Song came at him with the Brylcreem. "Just—just a touch, sir." With an ill sense of timing, in Song's opinion, Wayne looked directly at the reflection of his future father-in-law in the mirror and revealed, "Your daughter Grace and I are engaged, sir. We want to marry."

Song stopped and looked at the top of Wayne's head. His scalp had his face's ruddy glow. "Yes?"

Wayne cleared his throat and half-turned in his chair. "This is Song's Barbershop, right? Aren't you Mr. Song?"

"Yes," Song replied to the top of Wayne's head.

Wayne hunched a little and tried again. "Sir, we intend to marry." He paused. "With your consent."

Song understood perfectly well what Wayne was trying to tell him, but faking limited English might buy him some time. The less he said to the young man, the better he could watch him.

"I am a Methodist, sir," Wayne began again, rather carefully. "Grace told me I should be sure to tell you that." Song gave this some thought. No doubt the couple would have an easier time of it if they shared their faith. A white man and a yellow girl were going to need it.

"And," continued Wayne, "there is the matter of Mrs. Song's

approval." Gracie had briefed him well. "So I would just like to say that I'll take good care of her. I'll take very good care of her."

Song could not remember when he had last seen someone so earnest. The men looked at one another in the mirror, both slightly amazed that they were about to become relations. Finally Song closed his eyes. "Yes," he said. He tasted the word's little bite, its little promise.

For the rest of the day, the news sat inside him like a sprouted seed. He cut hair, lathered faces, trimmed sideburns,

all the while moving lightly, carefully, as though part of him might spill. Once, he looked up at the bright flash of a streetcar and realized something was flowering inside him. Mrs. Chin lumbered past with her salmon and Japanese radishes. She lifted the fish in greeting, the netted bag swaying from her arm. Song smiled, suddenly hopeful. It was true they knew nothing of Wayne Teller's family. But the young man had not expected Song's daughter to sneak out in the night with a stack of linens, half the family photographs, and a couple of jars of *kimch'i* as her sister, Sonya, had done. Wayne Teller had come to him; he loved Gracie.

Gracie would see, he would bring her mother around. Tomorrow, if all went well with Jungmi, he would run out when he saw Mrs. Chin and say, "My daughter Gracie is getting married!" Then he could rely on Mrs. Chin to carry the news all the way down the street, to Jasper Woo, who would be just getting back from delivering the teatime *dim sum*, and who would tell McCoy, the *miguk* who hung out in Chinatown and picketed all the businesses, including Song's, that undercut the prices in white neighborhoods. McCoy would tell Sampa, the old Negro bachelor who lived above the laundry, and who would shout out his congratulations from the second-story window down to the whole street.

But when Song pulled the key out of the shop door at six o'clock and double-checked the lock, he felt, quite unexpectedly, a stab of disappointment in himself. How was it that in all these years living and working right here on Ashland Avenue, he had never been the kind of person who would lock up at midday and go do something Jungmi or Old Woo would have thought outlandish? That was Gracie's word for a certain kind of daring. A blond American friend of hers had dropped out of college to marry a Moroccan prince. Russian astronauts had climbed aboard Sputnik to orbit the Earth. Out of this land, out of this world.

Once, as a boy, Song had been working the field alongside his father, when he decided to stand and stretch. He saw a gull sojourning inland, the white flash of the clay pots the women used during summer cooking, dried fish hung on a lattice of twigs. He stared so long these things began to shimmer around the edges. Then a *yangban* appeared, approaching slowly with his entourage—two servants on donkeys riding ahead and a young partner or son behind him on a steed. Song's father had told him about the *yangbans*, how sometimes they came around personally to collect taxes instead of sending their lackeys, and how the tax laws were always changing when the *yangbans* had a daughter to marry off or wanted to add a new room to the house.

He had been quite unprepared for the magnificence of this nobleman in his wide-brimmed hat with the topknot made of gleaming horsehair, his quilted white coat and lacquered button-up shoes. He stood and watched as the party moved past in a kind of stillness, made whiter and stiller by the backdrop of the mountains they moved toward. And then he watched his father watch the party, gazing after them with neither longing nor contempt. Even a self-important, over-decorated feudal lord was precious to his father, who would not live to see his country liberated from the Japanese. He saw the scene more simply now, its whiteness and stillness. Everyone, thought Song, is doomed to the present.

Squinting in the bathroom light, Song stood over the toilet patiently shaking himself off after urinating for the third time since he'd gone to bed. His bladder could not hold off like it used to. He had gone to bed before Jungmi had finished in the laundry, his joints throbbing in the damp summer weather, and had been too distracted by pain to embark on the subject of Gracie's impending marriage. The next thing he knew he had been sitting up in bed, trying to remember his dream, but recalling only the sensation of feeling himself a child again, contented, but untried.

When his eyes adjusted to the bathroom light, he noticed Jungmi's bright satin bathrobe still shimmering on its hook on the back of the door. He shuffled out to the front room and lowered himself into his chair. Jungmi was sitting up straight as a streetpole, fully dressed, on the sofa, her face as distant as a newly discovered planet. Something about the pastel terrycloth of her houseslippers made Song lift himself carefully off the chair he had just sat down in, kneel carefully before her, first with his left leg and then with his right leg, and take her hand. "Jungmi, please come to bed."

She would not look at him.

"The young man came to the shop today. They would like to have our consent to marry."

She shook her head. "It isn't for me to give my approval or not give my approval. It isn't my duty."

"But, Jungmi, there is no other obstacle."

She sat in the dark and she would not look at him. She told him, "It isn't for me to say."

Song blinked at her, puzzled, then Jungmi leaned to kiss him and placed a small something into his lap. He looked down for a long moment and then took up this thing she had given him, exquisitely soft and fragrant. White petals opened into his hands.

The next morning he rose very early, thinking that one remedy for his ailing joints might be more, rather than less, activity. Night had hardly begun to seep into dawn when he headed on foot down Ashland Avenue in the fog. The street was still so quiet he could hear the foghorns from the bay. Muted footsteps behind him, brisk but not urgent, seemed to be gaining. "Is that you, Song?" Old Woo called out when he had reached the park.

"I thought I would take some exercise," Song told his neighbor, noting that Woo's fists were pumping vigorously at his sides rather than clasped behind his back, as during his usual stroll. He was wearing white sneakers and a golf cap.

"Yes, yes, yes," Woo replied. "My new American doctor say, 'If you want to live long time, you got to pick up the pace!'"

Song assumed the brisk pace of his companion beside him on the narrow footpath. He had to admit that Woo was looking very trim. "Is it true, Song, that your daughter is going to marry, after all?" Woo inquired. "How do you Koreans call the white people? *Miguk*? Hmm?" Song gestured toward a park bench where he intended to sit and catch his breath. He sat. Woo bowed to him with a show of patronage. "Congratulations on your most happy good fortune, Song. May the obstacles to their happiness," Woo smiled indulgently, "be few."

Song sat watching a family of ducks huddled together in the fog, preening themselves and nipping at their loose feathers. This morning, the news of Gracie's marriage seemed suddenly irrevocable. He sat forward, restless again. What if Wayne Teller did not make a suitable husband, after all? What if there really was something odd, as Jungmi had suspected, about his wanting to be with an Oriental girl? A thought occurred to Song that made him stand quickly, scattering the family of ducks into the water. Then he turned his body, trembling like a compass, and headed toward home.

When he burst through his front door, he stood awkwardly in his own front room, his fingers twitching at his sides. But the next moment brought another sweep of courage, and he found himself marching through the kitchen, past the table set with the same chipped plates, and the napkins snipped in two for economy's sake, and the eggs gurgling in a pot on the stove. With a swift shove, the laundry-room door flew open and Song stood before his wife, who held a freshly laundered sheet with her arms wide. Before she could give it that crisp snap, Song grabbed hold of the bottom corners and lifted them to see her quick look of surprise. Her hands came together, clutching the sheet at her chest, watching him more with expectancy than annoyance, which gave him hope. There in the laundry, with the pipes hissing heat and the scent of bleaching soap scrubbing the air, he studied the face of the woman who had consented to be his wife.

"Will you give them your consent?" he shouted over the

spin cycle of twenty washers. He knew how he must look to her, sweaty and pleading. He hoped that she was not going to ruin the moment, standing there staring at him with her mouth open, her eyebrows two exclamation points.

She merely shook her head, as though she pitied him. "You the one," she told him in English. "You the one need let go."

They did not speak again all day. In the evening, he ate his dinner in silence, the empty plate across from him gleaming in wordless accusation. Jungmi was going to scrub sinks or empty lint trays or bleach sheets until midnight. He had tried to watch the news, but trudged upstairs, his head muddied by thoughts of those U.S. soldiers that President Eisenhower had sent down to Arkansas to teach the white people that they must not keep that little Negro boy out of school. He pictured Gracie riding off with Wayne in a loaded-down station wagon, headed for a place like Arkansas for all he knew, where it was probably illegal for the two of them even to be seen together, much less live as husband and wife.

When Song had first come to California, he began working in the orange groves and vineyards and cotton fields of the Great Central Valley. He slept in bunkhouses and rode in trucks and ate at long tables under the trees with Filipinos, Chinese, Armenians, and Japanese, riding from Dinuba to Salinas, Gilroy to Coalinga, Sacramento to Fresno. There were men he worked beside who had left their families, men who had lost them, men like him who were waiting for their families to begin. He avoided the Japanese, who were still the enemy of his people even if he sweated alongside them. Missionaries came out to the fields. Because it meant clean used clothes and free doctors' checkups, he converted.

It was eight years before he had saved enough to think of marriage, and eight more years before he finally sailed home to marry the woman his auntie had found for him. Jungmi. He could not return a laborer; she would not have him. So he had promised her he would enroll in school, learn an occupation. His chosen occupation never did sit well with his wife, until a stroke of luck came in 1941, when Mr. Toyomoto, the barber just across the street, had received a piece of paper from the American government ordering him to sell everything he owned and report to internment headquarters within three days. Song had gotten the business cheap.

They had arrived at Angel Island just one month before the American congress passed the great Exclusion Act of 1924. Had he not booked passage when he did, Song would probably have remained a bachelor. He remembered their first night together, his clumsy hands, scarred from years of work, and how he had felt himself going weak, weak in his groin, his skin sweating coldly, Jungmi drifting from him in the ocean of their first bed. Her sturdy, trembling body. He had thought of how the breath could catch inside a woman if she didn't know the country of her own skin. How, if she were nothing but emptiness to herself down there, any touch would feel like a violation. So he had taken her hand and placed it on her body, making the first touch her touch. In the first new days, he had watched her, wanting to get to know her from afar, too. She leaned over the deck of the ship, her eyes half shut, her nostrils slightly flared, facing the horizon. He believed she would come to love him, but she belonged to herself, alone; he could see that in her.

Pain woke him again toward morning. Beside him, Jungmi's breath was light and even, which calmed him. He felt, again, that he must move lest the pain overtake him. Not wanting to encounter Old Woo again on his morning jaunt, he started down MacArthur Boulevard. Already, delivery trucks were backing into alleys, and fish wriggled atop the ice in buckets deposited on the sidewalk. Song did not make the mistake of trying to outpace his pain. He made it past the Polytechnic and the public library and all the new apartments going up on the east side of the expressway. When he got that far, he began to feel a little better, and decided he might as well continue on to Berkeley. He would pay a visit to Gracie. And while he was on his way over, he would think about some of the plans that he had never seen through to completion, like writing a sermon he had been invited to deliver at the Korean Methodist Church, or starting up a Korean language school so that the young people would know where they came from.

He turned onto Telegraph Avenue and headed toward the university. Students riffled through the bargain boxes lined up in front of Cody's Bookstore or hovered around the kiosks that sold magazines and newspapers. Song noticed that many young women were now wearing their hair long and loose, like they were ready for bed. A young man in a raincoat stood outside a flower stall playing his flute. Song made his slow way through Sather Gate and across campus, past Berkeley Tower. On the square, a cluster of students listened to someone orating through a megaphone. The crowd alternately laughed or shouted something back to the speaker. Several in the crowd applauded or waved their placards. Song could not make out what the excitement was about, but people who were just wandering by kept drawing near.

He had seen it for himself, that white people had this pull. It wasn't just men like the orator, or men like Wayne Teller. It was their belief in themselves. It was their things. Their moving pictures, their streetcars, their two-for-one sales, their big wooden radios that played the Mormon Tabernacle Choir at 9 A.M. every Sunday before church. It was their tea in little bags, one per cup, their elevators, their shiny hubcaps. He felt it himself. He felt proud to be in the same *country* with ideas as good as these. How could a Korean-language school compete with all of this?

Song continued past the commotion and then stopped,

lifting his face towards what was now full sun. When he opened his eyes he realized that he was not certain where he was. He knew that he had driven before on the street where he was standing, but on foot he couldn't remember which direction would take him back to Oakland. He realized he was farther from home than he had ever been. It was not an entirely unpleasant sensation, but his practical side was beginning to make plans. You need to eat something and to drink something, his practical side explained, and you need to sit down. You might go into that coffeehouse where the unshaven young men are gathered smoking cigarettes and sipping from tiny cups and arguing. Or you might just as well go into the well-lit Chicken Pie Shop, where you will be certain to get food. So Song entered the Chicken Pie Shop, and his entire being responded to the warmth and the cleanliness and the doughy scent of the place. He was enjoying his hunger now; it made him feel alive. He would eat and eat and eat before he went home to Jungmi.

Inside the restaurant he spied an Oriental man in conversation with a young woman, her sleek hair tied back with a yellow ribbon. He saw that the young man was Jasper Woo, and the woman, a very pretty black-haired girl, was not his wife. Young Jasper's face was wrenched with sadness, utterly dejected. He looked as though he had been up all night. He looked so miserable he wasn't even bothering to blow his nose or wipe off his tears.

Jasper looked up from his coffee cup, and his eyes locked with Song's for just a second. Two things happened next. Song saw for certain that the young man was indeed Jasper—that it was Jasper—with a woman who was not Chinese and not his wife, hunched over a miserable cup of coffee in the Chicken Pie Shop, with a glistening rotisserie chicken twisting around and around just behind his back, and some change on the table between them. And in the very next instant,

Jasper turned his face to the wall, not in a gesture that shunned Song, but in a gesture that submitted to his will. He had been found out. Song did not know the facts of the situation, but he did not need to know them. Jasper Woo knew that as well as he did. Because it was not the woman who mattered, or the facts. It was simply that he had lost face.

Song could not turn and walk right back out without appearing merciless to his vulnerable young friend, so he continued to the end of the counter and deposited himself on a cushiony stool, saying very politely to the waitress that he would have a cup of coffee and a Danish, but that he hadn't much time. He learned that he could have the coffee in a paper cup and take it with him. So he poured in his sugar and stirred it until it was quite dissolved, and fixed the lid back onto the cup. Then he walked back out the way he had come, looking straight ahead, and let himself out into the street.

He found an out-of-the-way bench under a civic aspen, brushed the pigeon droppings off with someone's old newspaper, and sat down so as to cause the gentlest disturbance to his joints and his muscles and his bones. He let his breath out slowly. Again, he lifted his face toward the sun. "Cast the net," his father used to remind him gently when they would sit together in the rowboat on summer afternoons. "Don't simply fling it." And Song would nod, squint into the blazing blue above them, and then fling the net with all his might. His father would shake his head at him, but Song didn't know any other way. Later, the boat would drift under the shade of the paulownia trees, where the cove was thick with mackerel. He could hear the wooden clonk as his father lifted the oars, algae-stained and dripping, could taste the chewy, salty strips of fish his mother would hang out to dry. He squinted into the old, old sunlight, sweet ache of memory warming his bones.

A student whished past him on a bicycle with a transistor

radio blaring at his ear. It was one of the very few times in many years that he was not at his shop on a workday morning. The first time was the day he had learned of his father's death, by letter, months after the fact. Then the belief which he had sailed away with, at the age of eighteen—that he was going back, that he was most certainly going back—quietly died in him in a day. The second time was on a Monday morning in that same year, a few months after Gracie was born. It had been a day like this one, with dauntless sun. He had asked Jungmi to strap the baby to his chest the way women wore them. She had complained that he would drop the child and that it was improper for men to be wrapped with their babies anyway, but he had made her do it. Then he had climbed the steps that led from the second floor to the attic and from the attic onto the roof. Wind gushed straight at them when he lifted the trap door; he had to hang on to keep from toppling. Although he kept one arm around the baby, prudence required that he head straight back downstairs. But he had wanted to show his daughter the new bridge that was completed in the year that she was born, the bridge they called the Golden Gate.

Whitecaps scudded along the surface of the bay. Across the water rose the green coastal mountains of Marin, with their hushed forests of ancient redwoods. He stayed up there just a minute or two and talked to his daughter in the serious way that people talk to infants when they are alone with them. He pointed across the water and told her about a place that he had once called home. Gracie's little eyes and nose peeked out from the tightly done wrap and blinked, he thought, comprehending. This tiny person! He could not begin to imagine her fate. But here, just for this moment, he was never going to let go of her, this child for whom the whole world was nothing but a tightly wrapped cloth and his beating heart, and, above it all, this wild blue.

Tim Keppel

*Ah, the admiration of a little brother. This was back when
he thought the fish I caught would keep getting bigger.*

Tim Keppel lives in Cali, Colombia, where he teaches literature at the Universidad del Valle. His stories have appeared in the *Literary Review*, *Prism International*, *Mid-American Review*, *Carolina Quarterly*, *Florida Review*, and other magazines.

TIM KEPPEL
Earthquake Watch

A Place

In Colombia, nothing is certain. Not even the ground beneath your feet.

One, two, three, and you're the dumb kid in the class. Is it a freight train? A generator? Then you notice that the birds have gone mum.

This is no generator. This is the actual fucking *earth*.

You look outside. The power lines are swaying. A man in a doorway is hunching his shoulders.

Five seconds, ten. Next the sky will fall. The ground will part.

You feel it coming. You prepare yourself.

You remember where you sat in the second grade.

But the man is smoking a cigarette. And *laughing*.

This is Colombia.

A Friend

At the place where Lucho rents pirated videos, we drink a *tinto*.

Lucho thinks his time is running out. At forty, his youth is spent.

Last week one of his testicles was aching. He snores like an old man. And when he wakes to piss, he can't work up any pressure.

He dribbles.

The end could come at any moment.

A Woman

Catalina lies by the open window, naked except for her watch.

She never takes it off.

On the farm, there was no clock. Nor electricity. Their radio had no batteries. They told time by the sun, by roosters, by burros…

Burros?

They bray every hour.

And the watch?

A gift from her eighth-grade teacher.

A Place

I should have suspected when an acquaintance told me about a teaching gig at the Valley of Palms University. He said the job offered a lush, tropical campus, stunning, half-naked women, and great security. How about two out of three?

Last week the creditors showed up. They hauled off lamps, fans, even waste baskets. They emptied them first.

Lucho says he'll get me on writing subtitles.

I will become a pirate.

A Woman

Catalina takes off her dress and wipes her lipstick on a napkin. Her lips look smeary and kissed.

She's a market-survey rep, the company ace. They send her in for the tough nuts and she cracks them.

Today, an executive told her, "I could sit here all day and stare at your face."

A doctor with a packed waiting room spent two hours telling her all he knew about the tango.

A Friend

Lucho's house smells of old books and mildew and cigarettes. His clothes, everything, has that same smell.

"Youth is so beautiful," he says. "What a shame it's only for the young."

He lifts his chin. "That's why we want to catch them and keep them in a cage."

A Place

They say you can feel it coming. There's something in the air. The animals grow restless. The sun turns bright bright. A strange, chilly breeze comes from nowhere. Then, faintly, growing louder, a roar begins to rise from the bowels of the earth.

A Friend

It's Sunday, the day Lucho can't bear to be alone. Of course, there's his dog—one hundred five in dog years, his companion through the still waters of solitude and the rapids, named Rossana.

"For three months, she wouldn't let me touch her. Then one day at a restaurant she reached under the table and had me right there."

He speaks of her in hushed, reverent tones. Of her wild red hair and bawdy laugh. Her skin like marble, pale and smooth and cold. A precocious daughter of two professors, she liked to discuss Cioran and fuck all night.

A Woman

Catalina's tiny farm bordered a large *hacienda*. One day, tired of the trek to the creek to bathe, she went with her sister to see the *patrón*. Burly, gravel voiced, with a rugged, vulgar face, he looked her up and down. "Who is the beautiful *negrita*? I haven't seen you around here, my love."

He gave them permission to hook up to his pipe.

"Exhibitionist!" teased a classmate who saw her from the footpath. "You should put up a curtain."

Catalina laughs. "Curtain? I didn't have the luxury of feeling shame."

A Place

The evening news. Paramilitaries execute peasants; guerrillas torch a police station; and the auditor general is busted for "illegal enrichment," joining his four predecessors.

"Colombia," Lucho says. "Where everything happens and nothing happens."

A Woman

She shows me the scars on her coffee-colored skin. Medals of survival. This one, scraped on barbed wire. That one, flipped off the back of some guy's motorcycle.

And the one beside her eye? I immediately regret asking.

A Friend

Lucho is preparing his nightly meal: a foul-smelling stew of gizzards and greens, a hard-boiled egg… I look away. The stew is for his dog. For him, a grilled cheese. Any variance from this menu could mean chaos or even death.

"My ass is against the tombstone," Lucho says. "In a year, I'll need a car jack to get it up. The only way to get women"—he pats his wallet—"will be with this."

A Place

There's a custom here of saying "good luck" instead of "goodbye." Which is fine, except they say it as if you'll need it.

A Woman

We take a bus ride up to Catalina's farm: walls sprayed with revolutionary slogans, the charred carcass of an ambushed jeep. The farm is a tropical paradise—sugar cane and papayas, red-berried coffee bushes nestled beneath banana trees. She explains how the coffee plants need *sombrío*, dappled sun and shade. She laughs at the gringo who thinks pineapples grow on trees, who gasps at the chicken head staring from his soup.

After a shower, she hangs a mirror from a branch to brush her hair. A hummingbird drinks from a bright red flower. The silence, the shrill wail of insects, reminds you how far you are from home.

It was here that she grew up: no shoes, notebooks, or feminine-hygiene products. Embarrassing moments with her peers, but what's embarrassment when you're surviving on roots? All her father had to show for his toil were his threadbare clothes and nine kids who adored him but were desperate to leave. He was wise, good hearted, a charming raconteur, guitar strummer, and phrase maker: "I'm as restless as a dog with worms." He suffered all his days from the wrath of his wife. She blamed him for their helplessness. Coldly, resentfully, she nursed him to the end. On his death bed he told his children that his one great regret was having lost her love.

A Friend

"It's like chess." Lucho is recalling his days as a Molotov-throwing student, evoking Trotsky and Che, Los Rolling and Bobby Fischer. *Fitcher*, he pronounces it, quite convincingly.

"Commit an early error and it's irrecuperable. Your opponent will hammer it systematically. Even if you extend the match seventy moves, you have no chance."

"She gets calls from a lot of men," I say.

Lucho's nod is slow, knowing, Colombian.

A Woman

"What's wrong?" I ask.

We're at a concert of Andean music—one instrument resembles a row of bamboo sticks; another, a little bitty guitar.

Catalina looks fine in a black, low-cut dress, her thick, glossy hair tamed into ringlets.

When I touch her, she jerks away.

"It's him." She's shaking.

Outside, walking briskly, "But tell me who he is."

Even before she speaks, my eyes are drawn to her scar.

A Place

Blackouts, floods, runaway inflation, legless pedestrians knuckling along the street.

A red light means *floor it!* A green light: *watch out!*

Bus passengers trace benedictions on their chests.

White crosses adorn the roadside.

And on the nightly news, teenage reporters coming to you live from Putumayo with bullets whizzing past their heads.

Lucho raises his palms, his all-purpose gesture. "Your life expectancy dropped twenty years when you stepped off the plane."

A Friend

Lucho is reminiscing about Rossana. How she loved to lick around your mouth, then lap your face like a cat. Her tongue was rough and dry.

He's told me this before, but it bears repeating.

"There are times I have to hold a lit cigarette to my hand to keep from calling her."

A Woman

We lie naked with our arms outstretched, letting the fan cool our sweat. A tiny lizard is scaling the wall. From the street comes the clip-clop of a horse-drawn cart.

She tells me how, when she was five, a man came calling on her teenage sister. A man from the city, with two-tone shoes and a big yellow car. He brought presents, bounced her on his knee. He was to marry the sister and take her away. But he married someone else. The sister stopped eating, stopped talking; she was never the same again.

Catalina: "That's when I decided I would never suffer for love."

A pool of sweat fills Catalina's naval. I insert my finger and it makes a squishy sound. Her mother gave birth to her in their farmhouse alone, cutting her cord with a kitchen knife.

"Excellent job," I say.

A Place

The day is balmy and bright, the air laced with the sweet smell of rotting mangos. Girls in miniskirts buzz by on their *motos.* A lime green parrot squawks from a balcony. A man in a *guayabera* shirt is selling kites. And in the parking lot of the *Plaza de Toros*, several massive bulls are grazing peacefully. Or so it seems.

A Friend

That unappetizing smell of Lucho's stew.

"I've adopted a new guiding principle," he says. "*Preparado para perder.*"

He gives me a significant look, waits for the profundity to sink in.

Prepared to lose.

A Woman

Sitting in the empty bathtub, Catalina ladles water over her head with a calabash. "Stay in here with me, Papi, *sí?*"

She tells me how she refused the men who sought her heart—ranchers, *politicos*, even decent men like the eighth-grade teacher. That's why all were shocked when she wound up with *him*.

She didn't understand, either. *He*—she refuses to utter his name—was twice her age, a brawler, a bull, spreading his seed here and there, full of himself because he had "properties."

With his raucous, booming voice, he would yell out on a crowded street, "Hey, you son of a bitch, come here!"

He took her to the city, got her a room, and dedicated himself to keeping watch on her. He would follow her, pay others to follow. He sabotaged her attempts to study or work. Once she went to a restaurant with a prospective employer; he called every ten minutes. She didn't get the job.

When she begged him to let her go, he held a machete to her throat.

A Place

I return to my apartment to find a notice under my door: *What to Do in Case of an Earthquake.* It begins:

1) Do not incite panic.

2) Do not do anything without thinking about it first.

A Woman

She's eating a mango like an apple, the juice running down her fingers.

"Couldn't you go to the police?" I ask.

"I did."

"And?"

"They offered to take care of it."

"How?"

"Kill him."

"The police?"

"Well, of course, I would have to pay."

A Place

Falling rocks, faulty wiring, fans without safety guards. A bus full of Pentecostals plunges into a ravine and lands on a bus from the week before. An entire wedding party, including the bride and groom, is poisoned by adulterated liquor. And a man who walks out of a downtown high-rise is trampled by a runaway bull.

"I've been lucky so far," I tell Lucho. "Once a security guard was shooting at a thief, and the bullets went whizzing by my head. Little things like that."

Lucho raises his palms. "In this country, you have to be a cat with seven lives."

"Nine," I correct.

"Here it's seven."

Another Place

I come from a family of great stability. Rock solid. My grandfather owned an insurance company founded by his grandfather. Prudence ran in the blood. High-tech alarms, blue-chip stocks, support for an impenetrable Star Wars defense system.

My grandfather's house had a winding, *Gone with the Wind* staircase from which we kids tossed playing cards into the chandelier. After a dinner served by "colored help" summoned by a buzzer under the carpet, the men would retire to the den to watch golf. My grandfather had his own pale blue golf cart and a hell of a grip. In his nineties, smiling benignly, he'd buckle your knees with his killer handshake.

Never said a word.

A Woman

At the swimming pool, Catalina's bathing-suit top keeps sliding down. "*Mi amor!*" I say, discreetly adjusting it. She has no shyness about her body. It's a part of her, yet it's separate. Once, showing me a picture of herself, she said, "Look at that smile, still so sweet after all she's been through."

A Place

On the winding mountain road going up to her farm you pass a warning sign with no words, just a simple illustration: two cars crashing head on.

A Friend

Lucho's back on the subject of Rossana. "She's with some old fart now, some frustrated genius, I suppose. She told me she goes for two basic types: bright, successful men, and wounded birds."

A Woman

She began to see other men behind his back. Well, not really behind his back, since she never wanted to be with him in the first place.

One, named Gustavo, had business in her building. She wasn't really attracted to him, but he was kind.

Another was a "dreamy-eyed" Cuban doctor. To him, she was attracted. After a month of heavy flirtation—"There are many places to hide in a hospital"—she bailed out. He was married.

And then there was the photographer who saw her on the street and asked if he could do a "study" of her.

A Place

Not long ago a massive earthquake leveled a town in the nearby coffee region of Quindío. The city hall and the police and fire stations were all destroyed. A cemetery mausoleum was cracked wide open, scattering bones and skulls.

But the image I can't forget is of a rescue worker lifting from the rubble the rag-doll-limp body of a naked woman. Why was she naked? What was she doing when the earthquake struck? Making love? She had an astonishingly beautiful body, which made her death seem even more tragic, though it shouldn't have, I know.

A Woman

Then one day he found the pictures. Some of them, she admits, showed "more than the ticket." That's when he busted her eye. A neighbor heard her screams and scared him off.

A Place

Reports in the aftermath of the Quindío quake: a blind man risked his life to lead another blind man to safety. And the guards at the jailhouse left the cell doors open, but the prisoners didn't escape. Asked why, several unshaven fellows looked up from their card game: Because they appreciated the gesture.

A Friend

One morning I find a small worm doing the sidestroke in my john. I wonder where it came from. I hope it arrived through the building's plumbing and not mine.

Before I came here, a doctor in the States gave me all the proper shots. "But for what you'll be facing," he warned, "we don't have immunizations." He also advised me to see a dentist before I left. "Down there they have a tendency to pull."

"You have to understand," says Lucho. "You come from a country where people die of old age."

A Woman

We lie with our lips together, breathing the same breath. Her body is pressed to mine like a wet leaf against a glass. She's frightened, she says. I'm the right man but this is the wrong time. She doesn't yet know who she is.

We hear a thud against the window. We look, and see nothing. Then, stuck to the pane, a little white feather.

A Place

The aftershocks of the Quindío quake continued for days. Panic floated in the air like dust that wouldn't settle. People armed themselves against roving bands of looters that pillaged stores and homes simply because they didn't have walls. Others went around collecting money "for the victims." Funeral directors tripled the price of caskets.

A Woman

Saturday night I call and get no answer. Then a crack of thunder and the lights go out. I sit in the dark, calling at fifteen-minute intervals. The roof is leaking—big, loud drops. I sit so long in the same position that my legs go to sleep. When I try to stand, I collapse to the floor.

A Friend

Lucho pats down a yawn. "*Ah, la eterna monotonía de la passión.*"

A Place

In the news: The body of a man killed by the military is found wearing a uniform used by the guerrilla. There are bullet holes in the body but not in the uniform.

A Woman

He tried a new approach with Catalina, pleading and crying and getting down on his knees. When that didn't work he threatened to kill himself. And when the threats rang hollow, he drank a bottle of cockroach poison. Then he ran his car into a wall. Maybe not wholehearted attempts, but still.

A Friend

Lucho, always theatrical, is reenacting the scene of getting stood up by Rossana. He paces the floor, gazes out the window, sighs, checks his watch. He takes a deep, pensive drag off his cigarette. He frowns, nods resolutely, and resumes his pacing.

His dog, aroused by his antics, nips at his heels.

"Remember what I said about wanting to keep them like a bird in a cage? Well, what you have to do—and most guys don't have the *güevas*—is leave the cage door open."

He pantomimes a man opening a window, crossing his arms, and gazing out longingly. He simulates an expression of pain.

He's a good actor, that Lucho.

A Woman

Finally she calls, her voice cheerful if not euphoric. Says she heard from the Cuban, now divorced, who convinced her to go dancing. Also, the photographer is back in town. He introduced her to another man who wants to give her a "casting."

A Friend

Chess was his passion, Lucho says. He used to play day and night, in parks, in smoke-filled clubs. "In chess there is a beautiful order and logic you don't find in life."

He explained the different strategies: the queen's gambit, the end game, and, most important, the art of the sacrifice.

A Woman

Her town had no traffic light but she had heard of them. "They tell you when you can go," people said.

This confused her. She asked her mother what it meant.

Her mother said, "Why should I tell you when you don't know?"

This confused her further.

Her father, however, encouraged her to learn, to seize every opportunity. Swimming, he said, was a good thing to know. You never knew when you might have to cross a river.

The first time she used a telephone she was thirteen. She stood in line, observing intently, like a traveler in a foreign land. When it came her turn, she performed so flawlessly that no one could tell.

A Friend

"Let her go," Lucho says. "Leave the window open."

A Place

Newsflash. The guerrilla are massed on the outskirts of the city. A civil war could erupt any moment. And in Cartago, fish have invaded the water supply. You turn on the tap and little fishies come out.

A Friend

"You never know," Lucho says, "she might come back."

Then he raises his palms. "Sure, we've got our ass against the tombstone, but what can we do?"

A Place

The news: Last night during a domestic dispute, a woman whacked off her husband's hand. He scooped it up and raced to the hospital. Miraculously, the doctors sewed it back on. Now the man and his wife smile wanly into the camera. He's holding up the hand with a dazed, bemused expression, as if it were some strange, new gadget he has no idea how to operate.

A Woman

In my idle moments I remember how she liked to run her fingers through the soil of my plants, thrust out her tongue to punctuate a prickly comment, and sleep with her hair covering her eyes, so "it would be pitch dark, like on the farm." I remember the way she could be so stylish and elegant, steal the show at any party, and then sprawl on my couch with her legs splayed tomboyishly, exposing her panties.

She told me about a time when she and her sister, walking around their farm, two barefoot little girls, saw a big, grey cat staring out from a bush. But as they drew near, it suddenly hooted and flew away.

They turned to each other with eyes big as lulo fruits.

"We didn't see that," her sister said, "okay?"

A Place

I'm drinking rum with Lucho when the dishes begin to rattle. A picture crashes to the floor. A shower of plaster rains down.

"*Hijueputa*," Lucho says. "This is it."

I remember: *Don't do anything without thinking about it first.*

The wall begins to crack.

I look at Lucho. He's smoking a cigarette. *And laughing.*

I think about it. Then I begin to laugh, too, along with him, just to keep him company.

Merrill Feitell

With only our windbreakers and a single tricycle between us,
my brother, Bennett, and I take Central Park by storm.

Merrill Feitell was born and raised in New York City. Her fiction has appeared in *River City*, the *Sonora Review*, and most recently the Harcourt anthology *Best New American Voices 2000*. She completed her MFA at Columbia University and is currently working on her first novel, *Any Minute Now*.

Merrill Feitell

MERRILL FEITELL
Our Little Lone Star

The radio announcer recited tornado warnings for the following counties: Travis, Washington, Gonzalez, Gillespie. Terrific—except Audrey had no idea where in Texas she was. Was outside Houston a county? All she knew was that she was sixty-two years old and driving alone from New Jersey to Arizona to bring her daughter a car at college and, now, here was the terrorizing storm her husband had guaranteed.

She watched the horizon turn a faint, toxic yellow, then darken to green and go black. All at once, the bright red truck ahead of her seemed to vanish in rain—gobs of it spat across the windshield. If her husband, Dan, was with her, he'd already be rushing to an emergency shelter, somewhere underground with Danish and scratchy blankets and local authorities on bullhorns. Her daughter, Molly, on the other hand, would be joyfully shoeless, skipping through puddles on the shoulder. Audrey herself wasn't sure what to do.

Was everybody getting off the road? Was anybody? Audrey squinted and leaned and tried to see, but the rain was popping off her windshield, as loud and exciting as a fireworks finale. The world was opening. The sky was opening. She sat up in her seat and unrolled the window for a moment to feel the heavy drops on her face, her neck and shoulders, a quick pelting.

Glimmer Train Stories, Issue 40, Fall 2001
©*2001 Merrill Feitell*

Then the thunder began, seeming to emanate from the center of the earth and move skyward right through her. She eased up on the gas and searched for slivers of lightning.

And when those came, bisecting the sky and flashing steely light on all things, she realized how the cars around her had slowed to a crawl, how the lines on the road had disappeared, how even the trucks—the hearty trucks—were heading for the right lane. She was pressing her luck now, she knew.

But there before her were the golden arches, the first concrete thing she'd been able to discern in miles, so she made her way off the road. *My savior,* she laughed, *Ronald McDonald.* Truth be told, she was enjoying herself, finally.

She pulled into a spot marked *Customers Only* and made a dash for the restaurant, hopping puddles in the pitted lot. Inside, she rolled up her wet cuffs, bought a hashbrown and a Diet Coke, and chose the table littered with *USA Today.* From her seat she could see the whole parking lot. She watched the planes of rain twist around themselves, like sheets in a tangle, like a dog chasing its tail. Rain popped off the window and then fell away from it. It was erratic and unfollowable, like experimental music, like nothing she'd heard before.

"What is this? What's going on?" She turned, delighted, to the man at the next table. He looked up from a stack of papers to stare at the weather, the puzzle of water and wind.

"It's weather." He drummed his tan hands on the table and his wedding ring clicked on the formica. "And it passes."

He was probably forty, maybe younger. He was freckled and tanned with years of sun.

"So, clearly you think it's the right thing, in rain like this, to get off the road?" Audrey looked at him hopefully. She wanted to hear that she was doing it right, behaving in a manner the rest of the world would consider reasonable. Even alone, she was still steeped with her husband's warnings; he had cautioned her about lightning, breakdowns, and carjacking schemes. He had worked a long career in insurance and had developed a nearly devout faith in disaster, a deep belief in an inextricable link between calamity and pleasure. He'd shake his head in disgust at anything, even young marrieds in the market with party mix and a twelve pack of beer. She'd hate to be overreacting. "I'm not being wimpy, am I?"

The man chuckled and gripped onto the sides of the small square table. "I don't see anything wimpy about stopping in for a hash brown if you want one," he said, shifting suddenly to her, a challenge, a tease.

"No, I guess there's nothing wimpy about that." She looked down shyly. She knew she didn't look sixty. For most of her life she had looked somewhat older than she was, but soon after fifty, with the exception of her hands, she had seemed to stop aging. She kept her hair a rich brown and wore it off her face with bright scarves and headbands as though it was still the early sixties. *This is my mother*, Molly would joke, *Gidget*. Audrey was small and thin and had worn jeans and little loafers ever since she'd started the trip.

"Where are you from?" he wanted to know. Perhaps he thought she might be from somewhere specific, or perhaps it was just clear she wasn't from here.

"New Jersey," she said. "But not originally. Originally New York. The city."

"Well, I like that: loyalty," he said, and started to laugh as though he'd reminded himself of something terrifically funny. There was something easy about his manner, the steady shift of his gestures, as if a sway moved ever through him. "And what brings you here? The Great Texas Beanie Baby Give-away?"

"What?" she asked, confused for a moment, but then she noticed that the windows were trimmed with the bright small dolls—little lobsters, roosters, ducks—modern-day wampum. "Oh yes, the Beanie Babies. And that I'm bringing a car to my daughter in Arizona. She's in college there, a junior. So I'm just passing through."

She felt relieved. She had always been good with strangers. She was always nervous on her own, riddled with doubts, until she ran up against the world and was reminded of how well she could do with it.

"And now it's raining on your parade. How very un-Texas in hospitality."

"It's true," Audrey said. "I was hoping for better."

"Well, that's a wonderful trip ahead of you." The stranger looked up from his coffee and nodded encouragingly.

"I know," she looked down. She knew it would be a wonderful trip—though making the decision to go had nearly torn her apart. "My husband, Dan, had no interest in doing the drive. He wanted to ship the car out on a flat-bed truck, but my daughter was adamantly against that. At twenty years old, she thinks I ought to live a little."

Since she began college, Molly was so often righteous with Women's Studies 101. *Are you going to spend your whole life locked in a house? C'mon, Mom. I cannot even relate to you at all.* But Molly's disappointment had accumulated in Audrey. She hated to be bullied, but she was afraid of alienating her daughter completely—her spirited girl, her only child.

"I'm just going to go," Audrey said finally and calmly to her husband. She might have taken his hand if he'd been standing closer, but he was walking back and forth, gathering his shirts in a neat stack for the dry cleaners, his distraction itself a kind of dare. "Two weeks," she had said. "I'll be back in two weeks."

She had gone about her preparations with single-mindedness and silence. She renewed the triple A, had the car inspected, bought emergency fluids, and headed off hoping—hoping, hoping, hoping—she hadn't made a bad choice.

"Well, New York, New York," the stranger said loudly. "It's a hell of a town."

"That's right," Audrey nodded.

"Funny," he said. "Because I'm from New York, too."

"Really?" It was incredible. Sometimes it seemed everyone was your neighbor.

"From Schenectady," he nodded emphatically, smirking. "Good ol' Schenectady."

"Ah, Schenectady," said Audrey, joining him in his mockery, though she knew nothing of the place. She never really had that—contempt for her hometown—but all of Molly's college friends had it. Molly probably said, "Jersey," in just the same way, like she should be entitled to claim someplace better.

"But I've been in Texas for a long time, ten years," he shrugged and took a sip of his coffee. "Since I've been married. We're down in Galveston now, by the water."

"That's nice," said Audrey. It amazed her how people could end up in such faraway places—though here she was now, Audrey herself in a faraway place. "Water's always nice. Are you working up here?"

He winced, making a show of shuddering and screwing up his face like a kid presented with the wrong plate of food. "Am I working?"

"Yes," laughed Audrey. "Are you working?"

"Well, you could say that." He stretched his arms overhead and arched back over his chair. "I'm bringing a horse to my wife. You understand that there are many people on the planet, many people in Texas, who could do this with their eyes closed. For me, though, it's work. It's definitely work." He held up a stapled batch of instructions stern with bold face and bullet points

"Well," Audrey began cautiously; she didn't like getting into the subject of money. Her husband always assumed everyone had it. "Isn't there a service, a trailering service you can rent?"

"Of course. Of course there is. And they've got the dough,

believe me. Her parents' place, whew." He gave a low long whistle. "This is just a test. Just a test of me."

What did that mean, Audrey wondered. In the end, her husband was often right, strangers became strange the moment you thought you might like them. That happened all the time on New Jersey Transit. Perhaps this conversation had gone too far.

"It's just Judy, my wife," he continued. "Judy's sick—again. She's sick with something new and tragic and beyond diagnosis every day now. This time she's sure the cure is her childhood horse. So I get roped into driving up here, staying with her parents, trailering this thing, and driving it back. It took four guys to get the damn thing in the box. I just stood there. I don't know anything about horses. You know, I'm just some guy from Schenectady and suddenly here I am—the barnyard FedEx. That's me, the Pony Express."

He drank some coffee and then drummed on the table again. "You ever been to Schenectady?"

Audrey shook her head.

"The word means *Land of the Pines*. So you pine all your life and then end up here. I apologize. I do. But you've got to believe that I'm not the one to be doing this. I mean, look at this." He shook the papers again, amazed.

"What is she sick with? Your wife? May I ask?"

"She's sick of me. She's sick of living. She's, I don't know, sick. She's tired all the time. It's a while now. If I got in a wreck she'd probably be the picture of health."

Audrey looked out the window and watched a paper bag ride the current across a puddle. The wind had wrapped a flag around its pole and the wet fabric hung in defeat, huddled around itself like an animal licking its wounds.

"You know," he continued. "My parents have been together for forty-four years, so I've never even imagined divorce, but I think she'll do it. I think she'll divorce me."

"I'm sorry," said Audrey. There was resignation in his tone, the quiet distraction of defeat. It was familiar but still miserable to hear about a marriage falling apart, no matter how little you cared, how small your investment. It was like hearing about a disease, something tragic and unstoppable. He probably had no one to talk to.

"Well, I'm sorry I got started," he said.

"Please," said Audrey, feeling guilty at her own contentment. She was enjoying herself. It was a little like being at the movies, drinking cokes and watching the rain. Last spring break Molly had dragged her to volunteer at the community gardens and she'd resisted that, too. School groups had come, they had cleaned out the lot, dug beds, planted sweet peas, peppers, and strawberries. That, too, had been a surprising joy.

"What's the horse's name?" she asked.

"Carmen."

"Well, that's nice."

"Her daddy had a Ford dealership. From a long line of car men." He rolled his eyes. "*Car Men!* Can you believe that? Car Men."

Audrey laughed. She liked him. He seemed fourteen, a weathered and impudent adolescent. Troubled but harmless. That was the thing about meeting new people, you were always measuring the good against the bad, assessing everything they said and did. *Give people a chance*, she used to tell Molly after the first day of school.

She watched the rain beat at the window as the sky cracked with lightning, the electrified fissure straight ahead.

"Whoa!" he said. "Did you see that?"

"Well," she smiled at him motherly. "It just goes to show you it could all be worse. As miserable as you are right now, just imagine making the rest of your drive with your shoes completely soaked. Look at it out there."

She did have a pair of sneakers in the trunk, but still, what a mess. "Maybe I am too old for this aggravation." She crafted a frown and broke off a piece of her hashbrown.

It was then, so suddenly it barely registered—as she thought about her shoes, about rolling up her cuffs, about where she might get some fresh fruit on the interstate—as she thought about these things a sign, the metal *Customers Only* sign she'd parked under, whipped off its post, caught air like a frisbee, and then fell—like a guillotine—through the windshield of her car. Her car? Yes, her car.

She laughed, high and false. "Ah-huh," a two-beat chirp.

"Whoa!" said her neighbor. The glass on either side of the sign splintered and then sunk, a corner of the sign poking out like a shark fin.

"That's my car," she said, stunned. She slapped the table like a person witnessing brand-new technology, breakthroughs. "That's *my* car."

It was almost a relief, really. There. It had happened. Disaster had struck and she'd lived to tell the tale. She giggled breathily, like someone else. "I've never seen anything like that before."

"I sure wish I could buy you a beer," he said. "I sure wish we could take the edge off that one."

It was 10 A.M. She'd never been offered a drink so early before. "My name is Audrey," she laughed. She held out her small hand and noted the little line at her wrist. She had tan lines from her garden gloves and she was proud of them, the way her daughter used to be proud of the marks on her neck she'd get from the violin.

"Well, Audrey, I'm Trent." His grip was firm and his skin smooth but not quite soft. "Hello, my name is Trent, and I'm amazed."

When the rain stopped, it stopped completely. The sky broke with sun and the water began evaporating, draining, whatever it could do to so quickly disappear. A few puddles remained under cars and at the edges of the restaurant like a narrow moat.

The tow truck had come and everyone stood and marveled at the situation, how the sign had cut through the upholstery smack in the middle of the bench front seat; how it had lodged itself deep into the stuffing and springs; how the glass stayed splintered but intact on either side.

Trent insisted on following the tow truck to the service station to make sure everything went smoothly. "I'll keep an eye out for you, lady. I'll show you some Texas," he volunteered.

"How's the horse?" she asked.

"'In rain,'" he read. "'provide blankets.' So it's too late now, isn't it?"

"Probably." It was heating up already. The sun was high and hard at work. Audrey imagined what it might be like to live here, to go about the business of life with the sun pressing down like that. Maybe it made everyone friendlier, made strangers allies in the fight against the heat. *Drive Friendly*, instructed the highway signs shaped like the state.

"So, see you there," Trent said. He, for one, was friendly, smiling broadly as he walked backwards toward the other side of the lot.

The mechanic said hours. They could get the right windshield, but someone had to drive it over and install it. "We're talking five, six o'clock. If not tomorrow," he said, scratching his lips with greased-up fingers.

"I could just find a hotel nearby," Audrey told Trent. The rush of amazement had worn off and now she was feeling a little sick to her stomach, like a teenager in dread of calling home, of hearing, *I told you so*. She was a grown woman; she shouldn't have to feel this way.

"Well, I've got an idea," offered Trent. He squinted at her as if trying to determine in advance if she'd be game. "I've got plans to look at a piece of property over in east Austin. It's just about forty miles from here, so I figured I might as well have a look while I'm in the area. But it's a beautiful drive, so if you want to come along I could bring you back here later and you won't have to spend the whole day sitting around some motel worrying."

"I'm not worrying," Audrey said quickly. That seemed most important to make clear. She smiled and gave a brief nod. "I'm not worrying at all."

Though she was. She was already slipping into a panic so intense and so common to her that her daughter often chalked it up to biology, some unfortunate symptom of menopause that rendered a person at once jittery and distracted, sorrowful and dazed. Dan would always come up with something. He could review any situation and determine exactly the point where a person, Audrey, could have, should have known better. In a single sweeping assessment he could completely invalidate her whole trip.

She wanted a moment alone and some water on her face. "I have to go to the ladies' room," she said.

"Well, I'll wait," said Trent, all patience and concern. "Go on."

Inside the service station she followed a cool linoleum hallway to a rest room and a pay phone with a chair beside it. Audrey sat on the edge of the vinyl seat and thought briefly of calling home, just to check in, just to say things were fine. But the conversation wouldn't go that way, she was sure. She would come unhinged under questioning. She would tell everything in one woozy rush and Dan would end up worried and ranting. She shouldn't have to drive on with all of his skepticism prickling under her skin.

She could call Molly, though. Molly would like the adventure of it all. Molly was always talking about the people she met here and there, the whole world allowed access to her orbit. She would get a kick out of Trent. She would pull her knees to her chest and give a deep, long *Really?* She would respond like it was gossip and in a way, thought Audrey, it was. Here she was, a grown woman, a married woman, bumbling around with a married man, both of them far from home.

Perhaps she should just find a hotel. She checked for a phone book but there was just a metal cord hanging from the booth, dangling awkwardly, connected to nothing.

She called her husband. She had to. And while Audrey knew in her heart that neither the storm nor the windshield was anything to confess, she felt a tickle developing in her throat, a pinch behind her right eye, all of the usual symptoms of gearing herself up for an elaborate explanation, an apology. She dialed the number of her home, and with each button she pressed, she felt herself moving towards an avoidable fate, like watching herself pick at a scab or pull into a parking spot scattered with glass. *Leave yourself alone!* She would say as Molly prodded at pimples. *Give yourself a break.*

But here she went, the small process of dialing already snow-balling with exhaustion and regret. She would end up on the phone for an hour. Dan would get on the line with the mechanic himself. She would hurry outside to Trent and end up talking fast, making excuses, letting on that all her cowboy bravado had disappeared with the rain. She would see nothing of Texas but this service station. The whole trip would be over, amounting to nothing more than a bad idea. Dialing two more digits could change the whole day. *Give yourself a break.* And in the quietest way, thinking of her own mother and the things she'd never seen, with two hands Audrey hung up the phone.

She dialed her daughter's number, punching in a calling card and waiting for the tones. She listened to four soft rings and then Molly's voice on the machine, the frank, informal request for a message. Okay. All right. It was hard to decide how much to tell. "Molly, it's Mom. I'm in Texas." Audrey scanned the phone for an indication of where in Texas she might be, but there was none.

She looked around at the scuffled linoleum of the floor, the shiny linoleum on the walls, dragged her finger across a panel of it and imagined that this must be what it was like in the bowels of a stadium, of Disneyland, of anywhere from which a person might emerge and perform. She gave a laugh she wanted to sound light, casual. "Somewhere in Texas, and I am thinking of you."

"All right," she told Trent. Back outside she was all smiles as she pulled her sunglasses from her bag. "Let's go."

"Great." Trent drummed his stomach in a quick rhythm.

They walked behind the building where Trent had parked sloppily, taking up nearly the whole area with the truck and trailer. "Well, isn't that something," marveled Audrey.

The truck was a deep burgundy and the trailer was a sleek and shiny silver. The whole thing looked brand new and decadent, unscuffed and glimmering in the sun like a toy. It seemed hard to believe that a creature was living back there.

"It's obscene," said Trent. "When real guys pass with their beat-up trailers I can hardly look."

"So are you sure you can actually handle this thing?" Audrey felt playful and flirtatious, excited about the adventure ahead. "I'd like to be sure that I'm safe."

"Yeah, yeah. You're perfectly fine. I may be stupid but I'm not irresponsible." Trent threw the keys in the air and caught them. Threw them again, higher, and they crashed on the pavement, spreading out in a skirt.

"Can I see the horse?" she asked, picturing a deep cinnamon-colored horse, a shiny coat, muscles rippling at its haunches. She imagined escorting it across the great stretch of Texas, pulling over to a wide sleepy field, opening the trailer door, and setting the animal free. She hadn't touched a horse since she was a girl, but she could remember the short, smooth hairs of the face. She'd once gone on a trip upstate with her father and there had been horses. She could still picture her own small hand making the long, slick stroke down the neck.

"Well," Trent said, puffing his cheeks and exhaling. "I hate to disappoint you, but I think we should wait until later. She gets so rattled when you open the door. And I just gave her water back at McDonald's, and that's the most important thing. I don't want to get her riled up again. But later—on the way back." He looked at his watch and nodded emphatically. "That's what we'll do."

He let Audrey into the cab, and as she sat there, the fabric of the burgundy seats warm even through her jeans, she felt, for the first time, a creeping new fear that she might be making a mistake. She could hear Dan's cross-examination: *Didn't you think it was a little peculiar, a man refusing to show you his horse? Did you not think to take down a license plate, to leave the information—at least—on Molly's answering machine.*

What if her husband was right? He was, after all, usually right. What if this was plainly dangerous and she was too stupid—too busy with Beanie Babies and chitchat—to notice? She should get out of the truck right now. But there was Trent, turning the key in the ignition, throwing the whole rig into gear, the reverse tone bleating as he backed across the lot.

"Listen," she said. "It's very kind of you to offer to entertain me, but it's occurring to me that I should probably stay. If they do a bad job, it's my daughter who ends up with a faulty car." He should be reminded: she was somebody's mother.

"Well, that's the sad truth about these things. They could do a bad job with you standing right there, and they'd probably be right in assuming you won't know the difference. I do hate mechanics!" He laughed, his head thrown back and his eyes darting and complicated.

"Yes," Audrey smiled tightly, reviewing once again all the

instances where she could have—should have—known better.

"But I'll have a look for you when we get back," Trent assured her as he pulled onto the road—a main artery already.

In the passenger-side mirror, Audrey caught a glimpse of her own car waiting for care in the bright parking lot. Trent had them moving fast, up to fifty in moments, already accelerating from ramp to highway. He flicked on the radio and the truck filled with mariachi music, the tickle of guitars mixing their lines of sorrow and hope.

"You should just relax and have a nice look around. It's beautiful here," he said. "See?"

And it was beautiful—preciously beautiful—as though every sight around her was an extraordinary parting gift. The long grass around them was patched with wild flowers, small pavilions of color to break up the green. There was little but sky and field, a sprinkling of cattle, and the occasional signpost of a Texas flag, a lone star in the wind harnessed from flight. No one in the world knew where she was headed, she thought, and she might never be back. Her car might sit there unclaimed as she disappeared, by way of weather or misfortune, into some small speck of this giant state.

Or not.

She might just find herself arriving in Arizona in that punchy little Subaru only to tell Molly that, yes, she had had an adventure; yes, she had seen the land—and she'd been entirely too worried to enjoy a thing.

"You barely know me, and already you're telling me I need to relax." Audrey laughed, a self-conscious little titter.

Trent shrugged and kept his eyes on the road.

Granted this trip was exceptional, but even the simplest pleasures could be impossible for Audrey to enjoy. Just last weekend there had been spring fireworks on the river and, with Dan not feeling well, she had gone alone to watch the display. Dan had even encouraged her to go, yet, as she drove along the parked cars and the revelers lining the road, she had gotten nervous about finding a safe place to park; nervous about drunks breaking into the car; nervous about the police car behind her and whether or not the new registration had made it into the glove box or was still sitting in the kitchen by the telephone.

And so she had stayed in the car all evening, driving on through several tiny towns, past all the small parties along the road bright with hibachis and toddlers pointing to the sky.

She caught bits and pieces of the gorgeous explosions in her rear-view mirror and, on the way home, up ahead over the dash. And she resented Dan for training her to see the doom in all things, and she resented Molly for daring her to be as brave as a teen, and she resented her own preoccupation with pleasing everyone else—had she lost all faith in thinking for herself?

In the end, she told Dan and Molly that, yes, she'd parked safely and then sat right in the heart of things having an utterly wonderful time. And, privately, she promised herself to stop letting every pleasurable experience turn into yet another instance of regret.

She imagined telling Molly and Dan proudly about this day. It was so peaceful, she would say. The truck so heavy and solid on the road. Molly would ask about Trent, if he was handsome, if he was flirtatious, if he was, well, Texas friendly. Audrey looked at him. He had the uncanny look of a boy in a man's body. His skin looked tough but he was still lean and sinewy. She could picture him still—at his age—swinging from doorways, climbing over fences, getting too drunk. His arms were covered with tiny scratches and scars.

But when Audrey looked at his face, it was certainly interesting, certainly handsome, but it was just a face—a long nose, a sharp chin, a high brow. He kept it active, amused, responsive to the world, but it was just the face of a man beside her driving on a highway to a destination she hadn't chosen but merely consented to arrive at. This was just life, life in her skin, the only way it ever felt—mildly concerned, a bit anxious, open to delight but not quite immersed in it. A step away from that always.

She pinched her lips—such a foolish looking gesture, but something she had done since childhood when she was afraid, fear bucking about inside her on a dare as she put her head down to go.

"So where is it exactly we're headed?" asked Audrey, brightly and determined.

"Just a little ways down the road." Trent scratched aggressively at his head and Audrey watched his other hand drift lazily to his lap, his two fingers suddenly the only connection to the wheel. He seemed so casual, almost deliberately casual.

"East Austin," he gave a quick drumroll on the steering wheel. "America's favorite vacationland."

"I've heard wonderful things about Austin," Audrey offered.

"I give you fair warning, lady. This is not the part of Austin you've been hearing about." He smirked, looking straight ahead.

"Well, if it's so awful, then why would we want to look at property there?" She didn't mean to sound nervous; she hoped she didn't sound nervous. "You know what they say: *Location. Location. Location.*"

"Well, it's bad, but it's not that bad," reasoned Trent. "Or, actually, it is that bad—but it's supposed to get better. Judy's little brother, Bailey—my brother-in-law—he bought himself some god-awful piece of property there and he thinks I ought to do the same. But I'll tell you, when he bought his place it was nothing but holes everywhere you looked—in the floor boards, in the roof, in the walls. It was less like a house than a piece of cheese." Trent threw his head back, his chin high, his laughter loud.

"He wants you to live like that?"

"No, no. I think he just wants to keep me in Texas. He wants me flush with a backup plan in case Judy and I split. The two of us are like this," Trent took his right hand off the wheel and squeezed it into a tight fist, presenting Audrey the inside of his arm, the long veins pronounced and flinching. It seemed a scary way of saying they were close—intense and explosive.

"So you wouldn't go back to New York?" she asked. "If things don't work out?"

"No. I could never go back." He looked pensively ahead, his lips pursed as though he'd lost his train of thought. Audrey said nothing, she just watched. Why couldn't he ever go back? People were so peculiar. There was just so much history and circuitry in them, you never had any idea what was going on inside. She watched Trent scratch his cheek, his mind still lost somewhere on the horizon. She wished for something to do with her hands so she opened her purse and began digging around in it. She felt her wallet, her tissues, her eyeglasses case.

"Anyway," Trent said suddenly, shockingly, reeling himself back in from the distance. "Anyway, anyway, anyway—the house. Mind you, living in the house is just an alternate plan. A just-in-case. The real plan is something else. What Bailey wants to do, what he thinks he's going to do, is rebuild from scratch out of the Home Depot and then sell the place to Bill Gates or something. He says the neighborhood is getting better—but I don't think it's happening as fast as he thinks it is."

Audrey was always fascinated by gentrification, reverent of the people getting in at the right time. It killed her to think of the apartments they could have bought in Manhattan, but Dan had no patience to wait for a neighborhood to transform, for the risks to diminish.

"It's probably smart," she said, feeling nearly envious.

"Well, maybe," he said sharply. "Of course, I'd rather keep my wife than become a real-estate mogul."

"Of course," she said. "I'm sorry."

"I mean, there's no place like home," he said plainly, almost defiantly, turning to Audrey to see her response.

But she didn't know what to say. Did he mean no place like Galveston or like Schenectady? Or no place like beside his wife when things were romantic and new?

"There's no place like home," she repeated softly, though when she thought of home just then she thought not of the light, spare sprawl she had painstakingly decorated in Northern New Jersey, but, instead, of the small, dark apartment in which she'd grown up, doilies and oil cloth on every surface, the flat, broad leaves of plants gone caked in dust. She remembered climbing from step stool to counter top to reach for things to cook. Her parents had been broke and struggling, and she'd always taken care of herself. She'd told Dan stories he couldn't believe: at seven, ironing school clothes on the floor; at nine, tumbling off the fridge trying to change a high bulb. "I can't stand it," he'd say. "Stop."

She missed him suddenly very much.

Trent pulled off the highway and turned into a neighborhood lined with small, sagging houses on tiny lots cluttered with toys, bags of leaves, a rusted wheel barrow, a porcelain sink basin streaked with rust. "We're almost there," he said.

And while Audrey had anticipated streets lined with declining houses and beat-up vehicles, she hadn't anticipated driving beyond them—to streets where the windows were either boarded up or broken, the porches collapsing, the telephone wires dangling down. At first, they passed a few people out on the street: a small child in a diaper sitting on a porch, two men in blue jeans working on a car, one of them just legs poking out from under the hood. But now there was no one, no motion anywhere except a matted black and white dog, ambling slowly away.

"Is this it?" she asked.

Trent nodded. "Nearly."

She reached back into her purse, remembering suddenly that she didn't even have her keys. They were back with the mechanic inside the car. Even her house keys were in her valise, tucked away inside the Subaru trunk. She had nothing at all to help her protect herself.

She laughed, an amazed burst of sound. It was absurd, it occurred to her suddenly, to think she'd be in any better shape with a sharp key held tightly in her knobby fist. She was arthritic and there was really nowhere to run.

"What?" asked Trent. "Why are you laughing?"

She just shook her head and pinched at her lips, trying not to think of her husband's face as she pulled out of the driveway three days ago, how he had rubbed his eyes like a tired child. He did that often in frustration and his skin showed the wear. He did few things, and did them well. Investing, golf, protecting. These things. She loved him very much. She did.

Trent negotiated the tight, awkward turns until they were driving along the stone wall of a cemetery. Audrey looked at the assortment of stones, the small and tilting white ones worn nearly smooth; the grand shiny monuments declaring lives of splendor. It amazed her that no matter where you went, there were people who felt entitled to such spectacle. Audrey herself wished to be cremated, her ashes scattered, though she had never made any mention of where; she'd never decided. She liked the idea of the Brooklyn Bridge. It was one of her favorite places, yet she wasn't sure about landing all over the city—dusting the fish market and falling into the East River along with the soot of trains and buses, all that exhaust and sludge. It was the vantage point she liked, not the destination.

"Look," said Trent, "I don't think I can handle these turns with this whole back end. You don't mind walking a couple of blocks, do you?"

"No," said Audrey. "That's fine." She was thinking about everything she'd seen on the trip: Pennsylvania, Virginia, Tennessee, and Arkansas, the scrub grass and deciduous trees getting darker and thicker along the way. She had made it through a breathtaking storm.

Trent parked next to the cemetery and they both got out of the truck.

"Well, it sure isn't a very nice neighborhood, is it now?" Trent stood tall, stretching, rolling his neck in circles.

"No," said Audrey. "It isn't."

She felt a headache coming on, the distraction of pressure behind her eyes; it gave her something to focus on. The air was heavy and thick as though, despite the sun and the great heat, it was gearing up to rain again. Trent was saying something but she couldn't really hear. The overgrown grass outside the cemetery wall was a clamor of buzzes and ticks, the arguments of birds and bugs and frogs rising from the green. There was a cluster of rose bushes overgrown to a sprawl. It was a beautiful bush, ornamented with pink blossoms low to the ground like a Christmas tree decorated by the arm of a small child alone.

Audrey squatted beside it and pinched one of the many buds which were tight and full, just beginning to crack with color. They were lovely.

"You know," said Trent. "I would buy a house here if it

meant pleasing Bailey. I love him like a brother. I do."

"Mmm," she said, not thinking of anything but how long they might stay by this beautiful bush under this beating sun.

The roots of the bush were tangled with weeds and she began pulling out tight clumps of them. It was clear they'd encroach again within days, but she kept at it. She loved the tug of the earth, the slick rope of grass in her hands.

"There was this one time," Trent said, sitting down beside her and picking at the grass between his crossed legs. "This is embarrassing, but Judy and I were at her parents' house after a big dinner. There was delicious corn. It was so fresh. We had picked it ourselves and had a feast. Anyway, it was after dinner and Judy and I were kissing on the couch and I said something ridiculous, something like, *I could eat you up like corn.* I was kissing her arm and we were laughing. I was so in love and so nervous and she was so beautiful. Well, Bailey was about fifteen and spying on us from under the stairs, and he just started cackling. *I could eat you up like corn.* He has never let me live that down."

Audrey stole a look at Trent. He had his head thrown back, repentant, as he closed his eyes and faced the sky. She could see the sweat bleeding through his blue-grey T-shirt beneath his arms and underlining his chest. The sun was warm on Audrey's back—even the grass itself was warm—but there was a delicious breeze that shook the roses, rustled the trees, and fanned through her hair, giving her the chills. Her knees dug into the grass as she twisted the stalks around her fist and pulled so hard it felt like she was reaching deep into the soil, extracting something, a birth. She had already stopped worrying about Dan and Molly and where she, herself, was going, and so she had given in to the singular feeling of being focused and competent, at peace with the understanding that she was bringing joy upon herself. It was, in its own way, a beautiful day.

"I'd kiss her arm all the way up. We were so terrifically in love." Trent said. "I moved to Texas for her, for Christ's sake, and now I really think it's over."

"Texas is very nice," Audrey said dreamily, woozily, not looking up. If she didn't look up, maybe she'd just drift into a deep and perfect sleep. Or maybe they'd just sit here chatting forever.

"Texas is not very nice," Trent said loudly and quickly. "It is not very nice here at all."

Audrey closed her eyes tightly. What she most wanted to do was lean back, stretching out on the warm grass as though she was about to make angels in snow. She could imagine feeling the heat of the grass on her back and the heat of the sun on her front. She owed herself that much, she thought, as she began to recline.

"I'm sorry," Trent said. "I'm sorry I got started."

Don't be silly. Audrey thought she spoke, but she wasn't sure of it at all. She clenched a tuft of long grass in her hand and finally, feeling the cool threat of his shadow above her, Audrey opened her eyes.

But Trent was not looming over her angrily, raising his fists in torment and rage. Instead, there was worry darting across his face, and he was shielding his eyes from the sun.

"Do you still want to see the horse?" he asked, lightly touching her shoulder, bending down to her sheepishly, embarrassed.

Audrey covered her mouth with both hands, trying to contain her tremendous gasp—she felt suddenly desperate for air, like she'd been waiting all day to breath. She felt her lungs fill—so much air in her she could probably float. She believed it finally; he wasn't going to hurt her at all.

She nodded, proud that she had trusted her instincts, trusted this person, gone on this trip.

"What's wrong?" he asked urgently, but she held her lips tightly together and gave her head a quick shake.

"Well," he said, bowing to her slightly. He smiled and left it at that.

He got up and opened the driver's side of the truck and extracted a gallon of water and a bucket from behind the seat. She imagined the horse at a grassy river bed, stopping to bend down and gracefully drink. She imagined the cinnamon coat beading with sweat simultaneously dried and produced by the warm, weighty sun.

Trent walked between the truck and the trailer and opened a small door. "Come look," he said. "And then I'll just run for a peek at the house."

Audrey could see the speckled grey head of a horse strapped in place with a harness and leash. She had blue blinders on her eyes. Her nostrils were wide—flexing wider still—blowing their small, white hairs around as she breathed. Audrey squeezed into the space beside Trent and brushed her knuckles along the horse's jaw. Carmen was old and overweight, just a pony. "There there," Audrey said, laying a hand on the horse's face and pushing tufts of coarse, white mane from her eyes, like brushing back the bangs of a feverish child. Audrey reached around the harness to draw a palm along the horse's back where the hair was short and smooth, the skin warm and pulsing. Audrey wanted to get on. She wanted to ride.

"It's so important to get them to drink," said Trent. "But you can just about break your back getting water to 'em…"

He held the bucket beneath the horse's head and Carmen batted her nose around as she drank, but still the process was calmer than Audrey expected—quieter, cleaner, more dignified. "She's beautiful," Audrey said laughing, overwhelmed. "She is impossibly beautiful."

And it wasn't only because she was grateful and relieved and too hot to think straight, or because half the country had already passed under her wheels, or because her daughter was waiting in Arizona doubting that Audrey would have anything to tell. Maybe she did it because of the graveyard beside her, its bright white stones weathered flat to chalk, but she stepped towards Trent and stood on her toes in her small brown loafers to kiss the soft pink ledge of his lower lip.

She rubbed a thumb along his eyebrow, smoothing it towards the outside of his face, her skin gliding over small beads of sweat. He looked stunned and grateful and curious. It was very quiet and she felt small and teary and impermanent except for that moment of connection and pressure, that simple little nip. She would never forget this day.

They parted at Pep Boys where her car was waiting, finished, in the parking lot. There were well wishes, a handshake, an exchange of nervous gratitude. She drove off through the hill country of central Texas, through the red shifting tables of New Mexico, through the thick desert scrub growing out of the Arizona sand. She drew her right hand along the fissure of the front seat, the crack revealing the foam and plastic and springs. She held her hand there as she drove, as if to remind herself that everything really had happened—she'd dared a tornado, weeded faraway ground, kissed some kind of cowboy, and continued west, racing against the turn of the earth as it kept on moving.

VERY SHORT FICTION AWARD
1st-, 2nd-, and 3rd-Place Winners

First-place winner: DEBRA INNOCENTI

Debra Innocenti receives $1200 for her first-place story, "Acacia," which begins on page 69, preceded by her profile on page 68.

Second-place winner: MIRA BARTÓK

Mira Bartók receives $500 for "Water." The author of twenty-eight books for children, her adult nonfiction has appeared in numerous literary publications. In 1997 she used a Fulbright grant to collect stories from Sámi elders in northern Norway, and is currently writing a memoir about her experience, entitled The Oracle Bone. *The essay on which her book is based received a mention in* Best American Essays *of 2000.*

"Water"

Maria links her arm with mine. Even in this heat, she holds on to me, for that is the way women walk here, arm and arm, to show they aren't whores.

Third-place winner: RACHEL HALL

Rachel Hall receives $300 for "Saint Malo, 1939." Her recent work has appeared in the Beloit Fiction Journal *and the* Chicago Tribune. *Her writing has been recognized with a Pushcart Prize nomination, an Indiana Arts Council grant, and the Breadloaf Scholarship in Fiction. She lives in Rochester, New York, with her husband, Bill, and their three-year-old daughter, Maude.*

"Saint Malo, 1939"

She finds a taxi easily, shows the driver the slip of paper with the address—72 rue Godard. She is unwilling to speak, to open herself to a conversation about the weather or the war, for that is all anybody seems to talk about any more.

We invite you to our website (www.glimmertrain.com) to see a listing of the top twenty-five winners and finalists. We thank all entrants for sending in their work.

Debra Innocenti

This is one of my favorite photos, my father showing me how to bottle-feed a calf. I inherited my love of land and animals from him. The calf became mine, Sugar Bear, and she lived with us for twelve years before she finally died from cancer.

Debra Innocenti earned her MFA in writing at Sarah Lawrence College in New York. Her work has appeared in a number of journals including *American Literary Review*, *Prairie Schooner*, the *Beloit Poetry Journal*, *New Letters*, *Italian Americana*, and the *Texas Observer*, among others. She has received poetry prizes from *American Literary Review*, the Center of Texas Studies, and the University of Houston–Clear Lake's Gulf Coast Writers Conference. Presently she teaches at St. Mary's University in San Antonio.

DEBRA INNOCENTI

Acacia

FIRST-PLACE WINNER
Very Short Fiction Award

*T*his time was different. They had come to look for him. One of them used his phone, and both of them walked with him back down the hill where a blue Datsun had rolled then sunk into the ditch of weeds. Antonio Conti saw the swirl of flies into which her body leaned. Her hair hung over her face, and at her temple blood had seeped through the thin strands and hardened. From the road there was nothing, a thick mass of Johnson grass and bloodweed, a calm shirring.

"Had to be at least a day," the shorter man said, picking up a stick to lift the curtain of her hair.

"No." The sun was squeezing Antonio's eyes shut. "Don't do that."

The man ignored him. "Jim, what do you think? A day?"

"Not more." The other man stood on the other side of the car, brushing away flies from his face.

They all looked at her a few more moments, looked at her bowed onto the steering wheel, before pushing their way through the weeds back to the road.

"County should've had us cut the ditch earlier."

"They don't mess with anything out here."

Glimmer Train Stories, Issue 40, Fall 2001
©*2001 Debra Innocenti*

Antonio stood silent. His chest felt hot. He had walked out that morning earlier than usual to escape the dim festering air of his house—although he generally disliked the outdoors. But inside a smell had crawled up from the sink and from the dog shit hidden in the labyrinth of newspaper stacks. He longed for someone to make these soilings neat again. *Tidy*. The very word was as bright and waxy as his mother's lilies. But she had passed over a decade ago when he had turned forty-two; a week after his birthday her body collapsed in a delicate hump deep in the blooming brush. She had meant to get the mail and her heart failed, a stumbled rhythm, the blood a tight pool bursting through her ventricle. Lately the smell of starch brought a fresh despair from the expanse of Antonio's ample belly. It settled thorny in the back of his throat and grew new branches there.

He sank down. His pale, thick legs shaking with the thump.

"Hey, what's the matter? You all right?"

He wanted his heart to rupture, but it wouldn't. It kept clenching, but harder and faster so that he could feel it knock in him, a new alive thing.

"I wrote a letter," he said. "I wrote a letter about the ditch. It rained so much."

"C'mon. I'll drive you back up to your house." The shorter man did most of the talking. "It'll be some time before they come."

"We can't leave her here."

"She's been here a while already. It ain't going to hurt her."

"We can't leave her here." Antonio stood, scratching. He hated the men, hated that they moved and talked so smoothly. They drove the oily machinery that shredded ditches, they tinkered with bolts, hitched and unhitched metal blades. Josephine lay stiffening in the car, released. The world had spit her out, the way his mother was spit out, and the hot, fly-ridden place left behind shivered with their absences.

He lived by the farm road, a grey vein of slight activity; everything else was the hoary beige of late summer meadows. Josephine would drive down this road on her way to work at the library, most of her face hidden by sunglasses, her brown locks pushed back by the breeze. When he woke early enough, he would watch her speed by, cloaked by the waving acacia, then drive to follow her path. There, in the genealogical room, were records of the first settlers in the county, the stout, expressionless men who drained the Texas marshland of its viral waters and planted into the uncovered loam the first seeds of cotton. He often sat in the back, his legs barely fitting under the low table, and flipped the pages of hundred-year-old newspapers, listening to their calming creaks and cracks.

The library was always sparely inhabited. Josephine, who worked weekdays ten to six, would walk quietly over to him, her hands folded at her waist, and ask if there was anything she could help him with. Was there something in particular he was looking for? And he'd look up, trying to control the nervous jerks of his body—she smelled like lily of the valley, the scent curled under his teeth—saying much too fast, but, yes, still confidently, that no, he had it quite under control, this information he was hunting. She must have heard the stories about him, how he walked through his property without shoes or clothes, how he wrote daily letters to the *Mission County Advocate*. There was nothing in her face or in the way she tried to use her hands to cover her arms, but the knowledge seemed to invade the library, like it did the bookstore, the bank, and the pastry shop on the corner, and to produce a kind of humming that he imagined birds must feel when winter became a clear idea in the shifting gulf winds. She was in it, too, no matter how separated he wanted to imagine her. Neat and starched, the thick fabric of her clothes had shivered like parchment as she walked back to her desk.

In his sleep some days, he floated all the way up to the library ceiling. It was a new building, the tallest; at its highest slope was a series of skylights, and the moonlight was as cool as nylon. The stars which were piled in the purple expanse in strangely large quantities were as spiky and white as little mints. He scooped a handful and pushed a few into his mouth with his fingers, the flavor a cross between peppermint and ginger. It cooled his entire body before finally producing a concentrated heat in his groin. Josephine was a creature of mirrors. Her figure faintly lit the skylight glass, but when he turned she wasn't where she'd have to be to cast that reflection.

He would always be disappointed in the real library the next day. It was spoiled by the persistent ownership of gravity. He wanted to bring all of his worlds together. But they were stubborn things, and so he had resigned himself to two be-ings, two Antonios that he navigated like both sides of a complicated game.

Josephine di Prima. Her nameplate sat neatly on her desk, the black serif letters as formal as her straight-backed posture. Antonio would stroke the pages of the old newspapers, the same color as her sunless cheeks, and say to himself, "Josephine Conti. Josephine Conti." The Antonio who lived in the heavy world of wakefulness could not look into her face. The Antonio who dreamed under the shelter of acacia kissed her hair.

Antonio looked at the men, orderly and certain in their damp, blue uniforms. His voice was as definite as he could make it. "We can't leave her here. We'll have to take her up to the house."

"Oh, c'mon." Jim spoke loudly. "You're not supposed to do that. There's stuff they have to do. Check to see what hap-pened."

"It's illegal," the shorter man agreed.

"And I ain't putting no dead body in my truck, or on the tractor, for that matter. Look at it, for God's sake." Jim walked uphill to the tractor, opened the door, pulled himself in, and shut it hard. He didn't start it.

The shorter man shuffled his boots like he didn't know what to say. He took off his cap and wiped the hairless scalp with a rag he had stuffed partway in his pocket. "God almighty. Your daddy worked so hard to raise you."

He watched them start off in the tractor, the shredder it pulled leaving a roar of dust and bits of grass.

She was just beginning to smell, or he imagined it.

The sun was already pinking his skin. It'd be long to wait. The ambulance came quickly for his mother, but it took the coroner five hours to come to collect his father's body. Antonio wouldn't walk into the room, so he paced in the kitchen, then put a pot of water on to boil. What would he do with it? He didn't know. By the time they arrived, the water had boiled away and the house was filled with the sear of hot metal. The old man's eyes had stayed open. His face settled into the expression it held most of its life, wrinkled brow, tightly closed lips.

Antonio opened the car door. It had to be jiggled before it finally squeaked ajar. He touched her arm. It was without her permission, and he felt awkward. She was heavier than he expected, and stiff. As if every muscle resisted him. His legs pounded down clumsily as he began to walk with her, a few quick steps, a pause. He had to carry her like a baby, because the rigid bend in her waist made it easier that way. It was hard to not let her head bump his. There was the smell of her shampoo, but mostly there was the smell of something like mud and the sourness of decay. Her face was covered by her hair, so he needn't feel the blank gaze of her eyes. His house was at the peak of the meadow's incline.

Inside the cedar fence that bordered his father's land, the acacia was covered with florid yellow blooms like a parade float. He looked at that as he gasped his breaths. It crowded the bitterweed and wild verbena. Huisache, a trash weed, his father called it, even when he corrected him, memorizing and reciting a passage from the *Encyclopedia Britannica* that told how the French called it acacia and cultivated it for expensive perfumes. His mother had clapped quickly and smiled down at him—he remembered with another ache her tender, scrubbed face—and without a word his father turned from them, took off his work shirt, and hung it on the fence to dry.

He imagined Josephine was like his mother. He imagined her hands were always warm and rubbed with lotion.

Midway, he fell. She toppled from his arms into the grass. He waited to let his calf muscles stop quivering. "Josephine," he said in the pause, to see what it would have been like to say it. Then he picked her up again. It was harder this time. His muscles were tired, and he had to breathe more heavily. He took three steps at a time and stopped, then three steps. He tried closing his eyes.

When he got to the top of the hill, he fell with her again, the air burning his lungs. He panted until his side hurt, until he wheezed moisture from his lips, then he dragged her under the huisache and lay her on her side. The bees that pollinated the yellow buds floated over their heads. Maybe it was just huisache after all. His right leg pinched with a spasm, his pants were darkly stained with grass.

She was quiet and absent, not frightening at all, the way he thought he might have preferred her, what would have given him the courage to look into her grey eyes. But the dreamed Josephine wasn't the one he needed. Now the heat of day would begin to roll in, grackles stepping through the cut grass, wings slightly lifted, beaks open. The cattle across the road began to settle under the shade of a sizeable oak. He felt love in him. Not need, not that impatient whir, but a sudden flush of love. And he sat beside her body that was now cooling and still, and waited.

Carl Schaffer

*This is the only childhood picture I could get my hands on.
It's certainly a picture my wife must love, since she asked my
mother for it. I have no idea where it was taken, and of
course, given the circumstances under which I got the photo,
there's no one I can ask. Beside me is my sister Carol,
looking uncomfortable on that shaky fence, and I do vaguely
recall believing at that age in the efficacy of the rabbit's foot.
There it is—dangling from a suspender.*

After a long yeshiva education, Carl Schaffer attended Fairleigh Dickinson University and the Universities of Michigan, Iowa, and Denver. He has published fiction, poetry, journalism, and academic articles, and has taught at Southern Methodist University and the University of Southwestern Louisiana. He now teaches fiction writing and Jewish literature at the University of Scranton, a Jesuit institution. "Inside the Wall" is a section of a novel-in-progress.

CARL SCHAFFER
Inside the Wall

Zimmerman arrived on the *General Blackwell* in 1955, ten years after the war, seven since the War Refugee Act that had brought the last wave of DPs preceding him. He brought with him his wife, also a survivor, and two large trunks still stamped with the trademark of a manufacturer in Kovno.

"Kovno?" John had said. "Then he's a Litvak?"

"A *Polak*," answered Nathan Bass, who had served as porter. "A Warsawer. Like your father and grandfather."

"Just what we need," John said. "Another hayseed."

"Thank you," said Abba.

"Why have so many Polish refugees been sent to us?" Itzik asked quickly.

"They must think we want them," John told him.

"We do," said Abba. "We told the resettlement office long ago that we'd take as many as we could."

"And this Zimmerman," John went on, "what about him? Where has he been all this time? Why didn't he come after the war?"

Nate turned to him.

"Why don't you ask him?"

"I will."

"You will *not*," said their mother quickly as she came into the room. She set down a tray of tea glasses and cakes and went over to John.

"Oh, Ma."

"You will *not* bother Zimmerman with your questions, do you understand?"

She held John's shoulders with both hands and shook him once gently.

"Do you understand?" she said again.

"All right."

"*Ever.*"

John nodded.

And so he didn't; not then, at any rate. A few days later, in the synagogue, Abba told John and Itzik that it was time to introduce them to the newcomer. Zimmerman was sitting across the room on a little bench beside a radiator, leaning his back against it as he read, oblivious to its persistent banging. His black suit was wrinkled, his hat at a tilt and dented where it had pressed against the metal coil. John threw Itzik a meaningful glance: he seemed indeed, as John had called him, a hayseed. When Zimmerman at last saw them approach he rose politely to greet them, and, as Itzik watched, kept rising, growing taller and taller until his hat seemed to touch the floor of the balcony above him. Itzik stared up, mute as a golem; his own small hat slipped top-down to the floor behind him, gaping too. He was an enormous man, Zimmerman, with a great barreling chest, massive limbs, a black beard that hung like a skin of wool, and earlocks thick as cables which he wore tied behind his head under his hat. And when at last Itzik held out his hand and felt Zimmerman's close over his he could feel, through the coarse skin, the thick grain of muscle beneath; and he, at least, would not have dared ask Zimmerman how he had survived.

Their grandfather was another matter.

"Zimmerman?" he said when Itzik questioned him on their next trip to New Square.

"Aryeh Zimmerman," Itzik said. "Do you know him?"

"There were plenty of Zimmermans in Warsaw. When did he arrive?"

"About a month ago."

"What does he do?"

And John, in the other room, stuck in his head and said:

"Nothing."

"Nothing?"

"Nothing. The man's a *luftmensch*, the bum."

What Zimmerman had done in Warsaw no one knew, but here he seemed either unable or unwilling to find work. When a few months had gone by and Zimmerman had still not taken a job he began to be called, as John had said, a *luftmensch*, a man who lives, so to speak, on air, without any visible means of support. It was rumored that he and his wife, a quiet, diminutive woman with wild eyes and an unsteady gait, were living off reparation allotments. They kept to themselves in their one-bedroom apartment on Grove Street a few blocks from the synagogue, where Zimmerman came twice a day for services; she appeared only on Saturday morning and always left immediately afterward.

Almost a year passed. Then, for no apparent reason, Zimmerman began to be seen frequently. Mornings he spent at the Farmers' Market, shopping from stall to stall; afternoons he whiled away in the synagogue studying Talmud with the old men. In the basement was a large room called the *beis-medresh*, or place of study. In it were long tables, folding chairs, great sagging bookcases lining the walls, even a small ark and *bima* so that services could be held there when it was not convenient to use the massive, cathedral-sized chamber upstairs. In the evening the *beis-medresh* was always clamoring with men and boys. Each long table held several groups, each group arguing its own portion of Talmud. From the ark came constant calls to quorum. Everywhere children ran under-foot, shrieking wildly. Itzik would often find himself straining to hear his table's reader over the persistent sea-like roar of unjoined voices. But during the day, when Zimmerman came, only a few old men showed. They all sat together at the same table by the south wall and studied from the same tractate. All of them, like Zimmerman, had nothing else to do with their free time. None of them, especially Zimmerman, seemed to know enough Talmud to feel comfortable with the night group.

They were led by Emil Lichtenbojm, the former shammes, an old Lithuanian who had been around longer than anyone, even the daycomers, could remember. Lichtenbojm, who was related through his mother, a Wasserman, to the great Kodesh of Baranovich, had studied in the Chofetz Chayim yeshiva in Raydun as a boy and was a regular at the night sessions. He led the day group ostensibly as a service, but really, as every-one knew, for the respite: he was by then so stiff with rheu-matism he found it too painful even to hold onto a broom. As soon as enough of the old men had gathered in the *beis-medresh*, Lichtenbojm would leave his work, take his place downstairs at one end of the long table, and begin to read from a Talmud, translating, after every few words, into Yiddish. After a while one of the other men would try it, Lichtenbojm correcting him as he went along. Then they would discuss the text. It was not exactly the Chofetz Chayim yeshiva, but it was all the old men could do.

"It was all Lichtenbojm *thought* they could do," Itzik would say later.

Even now, with Lichtenbojm gone, the old men still talked about the time Zimmerman first appeared before their *shiur*. The group was just starting the talmud *Betzah*. Lichtenbojm was correcting an error in pronunciation: "It's *Beyah*, Plotkin, for the last time. Show some respect. The Holy Rebbes are discussing eggs, not crotches." Suddenly the broad double doors of the *beis-medresh* opened and in walked Zimmerman, one inch shorter than God. Without a word he took a seat at the end of the long table directly opposite Lichtenbojm, picked up a book from a pile nearby, and quietly began following along. For a moment Lichtenbojm said nothing; he only stared down the length of the long table at the new-comer who had exchanged hardly a word with anyone these last twelve months. Itzik, hearing the story, pictured Lichten-bojm's astonishment as he gazed at Zimmerman's immense frame bent over his book, looking like a broad shadow of all those thin and wizened white forms. The Litvak sniffed; his long white moustache, stiff as a comb, rose and fell. Then he returned to his lesson and read on.

Just why Zimmerman had decided to come no one knew. It was clear to everyone that he was unable to keep up with even Lichtenbojm's simple exegeses. He said nothing, always passing when it was his turn to read. At times he would seem distracted, thumbing idly over the long folios of his Talmud. To Lichtenbojm's questions he gave no response. Sometimes Lichtenbojm would see him rapidly scanning the page they were studying and, thinking Zimmerman had lost his place, he would nod to one of the old men nearby, who would point out in the columnal text of Zimmerman's book the line Lichtenbojm was reading. Zimmerman would stop, place his own thick limblike finger over the same spot, and nod to Lichtenbojm to go on. Then, with his back to the kitchen, from which came a constant, gnawing drip, he would lean intently over his book, sometimes so forcefully that the table tipped upward at Lichtenbojm's end. He would apologize immediately, his deep voice rumbling off the wood cabinets, and the men would hide their smiles. He was indeed, as John had put it, a hayseed.

About three months after Zimmerman joined the group, he spoke up for the first time. Lichtenbojm was reviewing a passage that read, *For ashes are always ready in the hearth,* when Zimmerman suddenly blurted out: When they're *considered* ready. Lichtenbojm looked up. On both sides of the table the old men turned simultaneously to Zimmerman, like a crew of rowers. Zimmerman, too, seemed surprised to hear his own voice; he coughed once and blinked passively back at them. Lichtenbojm asked Zimmerman to repeat what he had said. Zimmerman did, a bit too loudly: the thin door of the broom closet shuddered. Lichtenbojm looked at the text again, rose, walked on shaky legs across the room, checked the Yiddish translation, and walked back. Zimmerman was right. And when, Lichtenbojm finally continued, addressing Zimmerman, could the ashes be *considered* ready? Zimmerman replied: Rabbi Yehudah tells us, when they are hot enough to roast an egg. And for what purpose are these ashes used? Lichtenbojm went on, amazed. To cover blood shed on a holy day, Zimmerman answered him. And why, Lichten-bojm asked tremulously, does the Mishna bring in ashes, when only earth has been mentioned before? Because ashes and earth are as one, Zimmerman told him, as when our father Abraham said, *va'anohi afar vaeifer, for I am but dust and ashes*, and as when Job said, *va'esmashail ke'afar va'eifer, for I am no better than dust and ashes*. And the dust, Rashi tells us, is the dust we are reduced to at the hands of kings, and the ashes the ashes left of us at the hands of the hunter Nimrod. For Nimrod was a hunter of men, as it is written in the *Zohar. Truly he was a man of might, for he was clad in the garments of Adam, and was able by means of them to lay snares for mankind and beguile them from God*. And thus we see the ashes left us of Nimrod are the ashes left a man bereft of the highest element of his soul: not the lower soul of *nefesh*, which governs the body, for that is of water; nor the intermediate rational soul of *ru'ah*, which perceives right and wrong and governs our actions, for that is of air; but the highest and most sacred soul of *neshamah*, at one with the Shechina, which is of fire: three souls, three elements, enclosed in their wall of earth. And when the fire of *neshamah* is extinguished, when knowledge is divorced from action and action is devoid of meaning which comes from the Sanctification of the Name, only the uttermost ashes remain.

At last he stopped. His voice, hardly audible at the start of his discourse, had risen into deep, booming, plangent tones that filled the cinderblock room, and the closet door, responding to Zimmerman's resonant bass, drummed in its jamb with each emphasized syllable. Now it gave out a last rumble and became still. Lichtenbojm was sitting up in his chair. The old men, like dolls, stared at Zimmerman with permanently startled eyes. Even they understood that Zimmerman had not only answered Lichtenbojm's questions in relationship to the text, he had gone completely beyond it into the body of the Torah and the Talmud, and even, in the end, into the mystical tracts of the Cabala.

At what yeshiva, *Reb* Zimmerman, Lichtenbojm said finally, with new respect, did you study? And Zimmerman told him, At no yeshiva. I went to no yeshiva. Then you learned the sacred text of the *Zohar* on your own? Lichtenbojm asked. And Zimmerman said, I studied under a rebbe. And Lichtenbojm asked, What rebbe? The rebbe from Raczik, Zimmerman told him. Lichtenbojm sat up. Was this the same Raczik, he asked, near his own home city of Kovno, and was this the same Racziker rebbe who moved to Warsaw in the years preceding the days of That Which We Do Not Name, and who was lost in its fires? And Zimmerman told him it was. All that remained of him, and of his possessions, were the two trunks he had himself brought with him across the water. Lichtenbojm's eyes filled with tears; and seeing him, Zimmerman's own eyes filled too; and the old men turned from one and then to the other and remained silent.

"Oh, come on now, Itz," John told him. "You don't believe it *really* happened that way."

"You just don't want to admit you've been wrong."

"About what?"

"About Zimmerman. You've laughed at him, you've called him a hick and a hayseed, and now you know the truth."

"And what's that?"

"That he's a learned man and a *tzaddik*. You can't deny that."

"So was Colm Cille," John said. "But *he* fought in the battle of Cuildremne. He didn't hide away, and he didn't let himself be caged up in some ghetto until they came to take him away."

"You don't know that," Itzik said.

"Do you want me to ask him?"

"Don't. You promised."

"All right, then *you* ask him."

"No," Itzik said. "There's another way."

"Yes, I know of the Racziker Rebbe," Zeyda told Itzik. "He was a cabalist. He kept with him a small group of twelve students who studied with him each night in his place on Grzybowska Street from midnight until dawn."

"Is that usual, Zeyda?"

"That's the way it's done. When I was in Jerusalem there was a similar group that studied at that same time by the Wailing Wall."

"And how long did the Racziker group last?"

Zeyda looked down at him, curling and uncurling one of his long white corkscrew sidelocks.

"Until von Stroop marched in."

Itzik told Abba what Zeyda had said, and soon everyone in the synagogue knew that Zimmerman had been one of the Racziker Hasidim, and who the Racziker Hasidim had been. At once Zimmerman was asked to begin a *shiur* in the evening, but he refused. The old men then approached Zimmerman and begged him to begin a session devoted to the study of Cabala. Zimmerman turned them down too. They, however, would not give up so easily. Why not? they asked. Were they not all of them, after all, well past the required age of forty? That Zimmerman could not deny. Then did Zimmerman think that they were too unlearned, they went on, to grasp the intricacies of cabalistic lore? Their abilities, Zimmerman told them, were not the issue; the terminology of the *Zohar*, at any rate, could be learned within the first three dozen pages. Then was time the issue? they persisted. Perhaps Zimmerman felt unwilling to study during the morning hours, even though he was not, if they might say so, involved in an occupation at the moment? No, Zimmerman told them, it was not a matter of time. Indeed the Racziker Rebbe himself preferred to study during the day, which he felt was better suited for learning the Book of Splendor. Then if their age was not the issue, they continued, nor their abilities, nor Zimmerman's time, in what way did Zimmerman object? He objected, Zimmerman told them, because he, a simple man, was unfit to teach it. And at this, Itzik told John, Lichtenbojm rose and said, If the Racziker Rebbe did not think you undeserving to study with him, you must not leave these men wanting because of your humility. For as it is written: *Do not communicate the Divine Name except to one who is chaste and meek*, and again, *Woe for the loss of the meek, of the pious man, of the disciple of Abraham.* And at last Zimmerman relented, adding, however, that he wanted no other but these men there in their group. If they wanted to learn Cabala, well and good; but they must allow no one else in the *beis-medresh* while they were studying.

Itzik learned not to listen at the door; someone was always passing through and sending him away. But in the corner of the hall, to the right, stood the long broom closet, just wide enough for him to crouch in if he held his arms around his knees. Once inside he could hear Zimmerman's deep voice clearly. The closet had been built with three doors, so that the kitchen, the hallway, and the *beis-medresh* all had access to it. When Zimmerman spoke, all three doors rattled. From his right, the kitchen side, Itzik could hear water running through the pipes; from his left, where the hallway was, came a draft whispering through the boards; and before him drifted Zimmerman's deep voice explaining to his aged and awed listeners mysteries beyond belief: the great burst of white light that had preceded creation; the pre-existence of the twenty-two letters of the Hebrew alphabet, the root of all names, and their role in the formation of the universe; the magnificent joining together, like husband and wife, of the jeweled letters of the tetragrammaton that had through their union brought nothingness out of void and into being; the flowering of the ten beatific emanations which define a direct line between man and God; the great primordial catastrophe that had plunged man's world down into the abysses of the evil *kellipoth*; the incalculable importance of the Sabbath in restoring the world of men to its former paradisial state. All the while Zimmerman spoke, the water gushed hollowly, the wind sighed, dustmotes floated airily in the thin sheet of light penetrating between door and jamb. For the rest of his life Itzik would imagine the Cabala as a kind of box in which moved raw, barely contained elemental forces.

Itzik could not long hide from John what he was doing. Sent to find him when Itzik failed to come home from school, John looked first in the synagogue and discovered Itzik just emerging from the closet. Itzik swore him to secrecy with such solemnity John understood at last the hold Zimmerman had on him, and he was merciless. He had always taken advantage of Itzik's credulity, which seemed to him boundless; now he made up stories about Zimmerman, claiming to have heard them from the old men, and marveled each time at how the huge Warsawer seemed to stretch Itzik's already formidable threshold of belief. One joke John never let Itzik forget. It began this way: at times when a tenth Jewish man was needed to fill a quorum, Zimmerman would leave the synagogue and, without fail, return a short while later with someone no one had ever seen before. When Itzik asked Zeyda how he did it Zeyda answered shortly, "It's a gift." He had meant, of course, simply that Zimmerman had an eye for assimilated Jews, but when Itzik asked John, John told him that Zimmerman *made* them, like golems, downstairs in the basement: He molded a special dirt into a clayey figure and carved *emes*—truth—onto its forehead, which immediately brought it to life. When the man was no longer needed he rubbed out the first letter, an aleph, so that it spelled *mes*—he is dead—and the man crumbled again into dust. John had even shown Itzik where it was done. In the basement kitchen, at a hidden spot in the back wall just beyond the trap door leading down into the storeroom, he opened a small rectangular door that Itzik learned only much later was an old milk drop. Sure enough, on the foot or so of ground between the synagogue and the newer building next door, there rose a mound of fresh earth! Itzik gasped audibly; John looked at his brother in astonishment and broke out laughing even as Itzik, realizing the truth, blushed furiously. John would remind Itzik of it constantly in the next few weeks, beginning with the very next day: returning home from school, Itzik found that John had altered an Army recruiting poster pasted onto their building—Uncle Sam now had *payes* and a wide-brimmed, black Hasidic hat, and underneath ran the new inscription: ZIMMERMAN MAKES MEN!

That he had remade the old men in the synagogue could hardly be denied. Not only were they learning the *Zohar*, but since, as Zimmerman explained, Cabala makes clear to us the reasons why we follow the seemingly endless day-to-day rituals of the Torah, the group studied the Talmudic texts Lichtenbojm had patiently read through with them with new dedication. Zimmerman included even the commentators Lichtenbojm had thought too difficult for them: Rashi, Rambam, Onkelos, all the long and convoluted marginalia crucial to the understanding of *torah sheh-ba'al peh*, oral law. In short time some of the old men began appearing at night too. And Lichtenbojm, seeing he was not needed, began making excuses and soon stayed upstairs altogether.

"That was what did old Lichtenbojm in," John would say later.

"What, you blame Zimmerman for what happened to Lichtenbojm?"

"Sure," John told Abba. "As soon as Zimmerman showed, the old man knew his day was over."

It was true, Itzik knew. Lichtenbojm began to fail soon after. When the old shammes was admitted to the hospital, Zimmerman offered to take care of the synagogue until he returned. The congregation was grateful, of course, but no one expected Zimmerman to do much. Zimmerman surprised everyone, going well beyond the cursory dusting and sweeping that had occupied Lichtenbojm. All day Zimmerman scrubbed floors, polished silver, dusted cabinets, arranged bookshelves. With a rag and bucket in hand he opened drawers, lifted mats, scanned cracks and crevices everywhere, looking for old dirt in secret places. Itzik saw him take a toothbrush to the rams' horns, dark with grit, until the pale inner skins were rubbed raw. He saw him wash away years-old dust from the circular window set high on the east wall over the ark, balancing the while on a long wooden ladder with round rungs that groaned under him. Seeing this enormous man attend to the endless housework of the synagogue always amazed Itzik; he would return again and again to watch. To him it was as if some great natural force had been tamed. And he remembered the night he had returned to the empty synagogue to see Zimmerman, across the room, mending the frayed corner of the ark curtain by the thin light of a lamp directly behind him. In the shadows, Zimmerman looked like some huge squatting beast patiently working a thorn out of its paw.

It became clear very soon that Zimmerman intended to put the synagogue, long neglected by the aged and ailing Lichtenbojm, back into good repair. He mended broken bench backs and chair legs, planed down stuck doors, fixed cabinets; he rewired the blackened-out rows of memorial lights along the back wall and silenced permanently the taped and leaking kitchen plumbing. In time, he would paint the entire synagogue, including all four of the onion-shaped domes atop the turrets; and of course, there was the wall, the seventy-foot-long, ten-foot-high brick wall that Zimmerman would build to enclose forever the courtyard of the synagogue.

"That was what did it for John," Abba would say later. "The wall. That's what brought him around."

"Around to *what?*" John called out from the kitchen.

"Around to the fact," Abba continued to Nathan Bass, to whom he was talking at the time, "that he was a Jew."

Meanwhile Zimmerman did not forget Lichtenbojm. During the month he was in the hospital Zimmerman visited him every day, bringing him kosher foods, helping him with his phylacteries, reading to him. Abba brought Itzik and John with him one morning to visit and they found Zimmerman already there, sitting beside him in a little metal chair as he read to him from a clothbound book engraved in gold with the title *Letters of Our Father Abraham*:

When our father Abraham, may he rest in peace, came,
    he looked, and he saw, and at last understood,
    and then he delved, and he engraved, and he carved,
    and thus came unto his hand the Creation,
    as it is written: "the souls they formed in Haran."
And then before him appeared the Master of all Creation
    —may His name be blessed forever—and
    He set him on his lap, and
    He kissed him on his head, and
    He called him Abraham, my beloved Abraham,
    and made a covenant with him, forever, and with his
        descendants,
    as it is said, "And he believed in The Name, and He deemed
        it righteousness."

And He made a covenant with Abraham
  between the ten fingers of his hands,
    and this is the covenant of the tongue,
  and between the ten toes of his feet,
    and this is the covenant of circumcision,
And He tied the twenty-two letters of the Torah to his tongue
And thus revealed to him His mystery.
He drew them in water,
He scorched them in fire,
He shook them with wind,
He kindled them among the seven stars and
  guided them through the twelve constellations.

As they approached, Itzik could see at Zimmerman's feet a large bottle filled with water, from the top of which ran a long clear tube that passed over the bars of Lichtenbojm's bed and under a small square of white bandage taped onto his chest. As they came closer Lichtenbojm saw them, raised himself slightly, and coughed. The bottle water erupted in small bubbles. From an open tube protruding from the top came a low hiss. During the next half hour Itzik could not take his eyes off the bottle. Each time Lichtenbojm coughed, the water churned; each time, Itzik thought, the bubbles seemed smaller, fewer. Itzik did not need to see the look of exaggerated indifference on both Abba's and Zimmerman's faces to know that it was only a matter of time. And when Lichtenbojm did, indeed, die a month later, Itzik knew how the old Litvak had left the world: through the great glass bottle, in a last bubble of breath too tiny, perhaps, even to be seen. He imagined Lichtenbojm's awful end: the long squeezing out, the slow lifting, the soft liquid pop as he finally struck surface!

Zimmerman said the kaddish for him, since Lichtenbojm had left no survivors, and after the week of mourning had ended he became officially the synagogue shammes and moved with his wife into Lichtenbojm's old apartment above the bathhouse. That, in the end, was what made him decide to build the wall. He had noticed too many strangers, he complained at the weekly post-Sabbath business meeting, passing through the courtyard. Was that a problem? the rabbi asked him. Along the side of the building, Zimmerman reminded him, ran a fire escape that led to all rooms inside, including his own apartment. Furthermore, Zimmerman pointed out, neighborhood children played handball against the bathhouse wall. The lower windows were painted black, but Zimmerman still thought it improper; besides, when the wall was hit the whole building resounded. His wife's nerves, he said, could not stand the continual pounding. At that the rabbi demurred; with a wave of his hand, he told Zimmerman to do whatever was necessary. Then he and the men moved on to other business.

The next day, John and Itzik came upon a stack of bricks and a trough of mortar beside the bathhouse stoop. Zimmerman, kneeling, was already on the third row of a long brick wall. This, then, was his solution. John and Itzik joined the crowd of neighborhood children who had come to see this most incongruous of pictures: a giant, in an old black suit and flat Hasidic hat, laying bricks. By the time they arrived Zimmerman's faded and wrinkled clothes were already smudged with new mortar. All through the day John and Itzik and the other children watched Zimmerman slap down mortar, lay down a brick, level it by a thread he had strung up between the buildings, and return the excess mortar to a bent-over, sawed-off snow shovel he used for a hod. He worked quickly, deliberately, expertly. Itzik could not understand it.

"Yes," his grandfather said. "This rings a bell. I seem to recall now hearing of a Zimmerman who was a bricklayer.

That was how he got his *ausweiss*, his work permit, in the ghetto days."

"But I thought—wasn't Zimmerman one of the Racziker's people!" Itzik protested.

"And what of that? In those types of cabals each disciple is expected to have a trade. Shmuel Nissan, for example, who I knew in Jerusalem—he was a jeweler. Chayim Bilauer, I remember, was a cooper. Zimmerman, it seems, was a bricklayer."

"You said they had to have a trade. Why? What does bricklaying have to do with Cabala?"

"To ask that, Itzik-Betzalel, is not to understand that everything in this lower world is directly connected to the world above. It used to be said of one of the thirty-six hidden saints, a simple cobbler, that with every stitch he sewed, he joined together a portion of heaven and earth."

Itzik's eyes opened wide; John looked cynically at Zeyda and clucked his tongue.

"Gramps, are you making out Zimmerman to be some kind of a saint?"

"No, but some would say so," Zeyda answered, unperturbed. "The Zimmerman I heard of made a living building false walls into apartments. When they came for the selections, you would hide behind the wall and the place would look empty."

"Why didn't they *fight*?" John said.

"Rabbi Yose once said, Yehudah, that when death is raging in the world, the prudent man hides; for once the avenging angel has been given leave to destroy, he will annihilate whomsoever he chooses."

"In other words, you hid too."

"I hid, yes. I'm not ashamed of it."

"Behind a false wall, Zeyda?" Itzik asked.

"Not quite. This is what happened. When they came around

during the first selections, our neighbor, a policeman, warned us. What could we do? I had dysentery. I was so weak from dehydration I could barely move from my bed, let alone chance selection. So your grandmother, may she rest in peace, did this: she put a little table in front of our bedroom door with a basin of dirty water on it, and over it she hung a plant. When the Germans came, they thought the door led to a closet and passed it by."

Itzik stared openmouthed at Zeyda; John was unimpressed. "Why didn't they look in the *closet?*" he asked.

After a fortnight Zimmerman had at last completed his wall, ten feet by seventy. He looked at his work, and saw that it was good. Then he picked up his trowel and his homemade hod, placed them both in a wheelbarrow with the remaining bricks and mortar, and went inside.

The wall did, as Zimmerman intended, keep outsiders away. Passersby stopped passing through; the ubiquitous winos moved on and found other places to sleep; the handball games stopped entirely. But there were those in the neighborhood who had not given up. A few days later Zimmerman walked outside to find the wall scrawled over with obscenities in chalk and stoneflake and, worse, crayon, written in the clumsy awkward hand of young children. Almost all of them were signed, and with names that defied understanding: Raul, Emilio, Georgie Gee, Duji, Yolanda, Carol Anne, Bubba, Bertie, Aldo, Paul, Miguel, Wolfie, John, Patricia, Antonio, Smitty, Sugarman, Bootsie, Expressway, Rico, Rosco, Bosco, Tommy, Annie-O, Knuckles, Chun King, Dozer, Booboo, Sodahead, Popeye, Ju-Ju Bead, Axel. And Zimmerman, who had explained only last month to the old men the multitude of names that had allowed all things of creation to wink one by one into existence, and who had described the ascent of Rabbi Nehunya ben Hakkanah and his naming of all the myriads of angels who guarded the seven gates of the seven palaces aligned under the Holy Throne, could now only stand blankly before his new wall in utter bewilderment.

After a few minutes he went inside, found a bucket and scrub brush, and patiently cleaned the writing off. A few days later, however, the bricks were again covered over, and again Zimmerman, undaunted, unruffled, labored with brush and bucket, washing his wall clean. Three more times this happened, and three more times Zimmerman without complaint removed the stone and chalk and crayon from the surface of the wall. It was a labor that promised to repeat itself over and over again, a ritual, like so many others, without purpose or outcome. But after a month of this had passed Zimmerman came downstairs one morning from his apartment over the bathhouse and found that, this time, the demons had used *paint*: the entire wall was still wet, covered with bursts of bent and twisted letters swimming in new colors. No water would wash this clean; no scrubbing would bring back the new brick's innocent silence. At once Zimmerman ran inside, appearing a few minutes later with paint, bucket, and brush, and began furiously covering the wall over with a dull lustreless red paint, the color of old apples, the color he had painted the great turreted domes topping the synagogue. All day long he painted. And when he was done, this time he did not return inside. He put down the bucket, lifted himself up, and just stood there.

"He stood there *waiting*," Itzik told Nate.

"Waiting? For what?"

"For them to return."

"Not *them*," John told Itzik.

"And what happened then?" Nate asked.

"We waited too."

They waited behind a corner for the rest of the afternoon, until the sun sank low in the sky and the topmost windows of the tenements surrounding them glanced gold. And then a voice called out from the third floor of the bathhouse: Zimmerman's wife's voice, high, thin, and wavering. Zimmerman hurried inside; a moment later John ran out from behind the corner, dabbed on the wall with his forefinger, and ran back. When Zimmerman returned a few minutes later, he found, smeared onto the new paint:

THIS WALL
IN ITS
SEVENTH PRINTING

Zimmerman was furious. He grabbed the paintbrush, whirled around, rose to his full height, and searched. The boys looked at Zimmerman with new eyes. This was not the same man who eighteen months before had arrived fresh off the *General Blackwell*. He now stood erect, straight as a soldier, his arms crossed, the paintbrush still dripping in his right hand. His suit, once whitened with mortar, shone dully with red paint that looked, Itzik whispered to John as they watched, disturbingly like smeared blood; Itzik wondered if Zimmerman had not been some kind of commando. John added, not kindly, that that was likely, since he had covered himself all over with the colors of Poland. Itzik, outraged, told John he would never dare make a remark like that in front of Zimmerman, and John laughed and said he would step out now, that very moment, if Itzik wanted.

"He thought Zimmerman was some kind of a *soldier*," John explained later.

"And why not?" Zeyda had said. "The Zimmerman I heard of fought with the freedom fighters in the revolt."

"Zimmerman!" John said. "Zimmerman was in the Warsaw uprising?"

"He was with the Jewish Fighting Organization."

"*Fighting* organization?" John asked.

"Yes. They were a group of Jewish patriots led by a boy named Anielewicz."

"A boy?" Itzik said.

"Practically. They called him 'Aniolek'—Little Angel."

"And the Zimmerman you know of, he was with them?" John asked.

"From the first battle, on Zamenhoff and Mila."

"Where?" Itzik said.

"Here," Zeyda said. "Let me show you."

From the edge of the table he took a newly made sponge cake and the butter knife beside it. He ran the knife over the brown crust. "Von Stroop entered the ghetto here, at the Nalewki gate." A gold flower bloomed at the top right corner of the cake. "It was April 19th, the day before Hitler's birthday. Von Stroop wanted to make him a present of Warsaw's Jews. There were battalions in full array, panzer cars, machine guns. They marched down Nalewki, toward Muranowska, Mila, Kupiecka, Franciszkanska...." The gold flower grew a gold stem, the gold stem eight gold limbs. "...toward what was called the Wild Ghetto, where those who weren't registered as workers lived secretly. At Nalewki Franciszkanska became Gesia. A short distance down Gesia it converged on Zamenhoff...." Another gold line began its way upwards, forming a gridwork. "And here, at Mila, the battle began." Three horizontal lines up he stuck the knife in. It clanked against the metal bottom of the cakepan and stood straight up. "When the German column reached Mila Street they were fired on from three sides: from Mila and from both sides of Zamenhoff. The lead tank blew up. The Germans and Ukrainians scattered. Warsawers came out of hiding everywhere to cheer."

"And Zimmerman was there?" John asked.

"It was a Zimmerman, I've heard, who threw the fire bomb that knocked out the lead tank."

John looked at his grandfather, absolutely silent.

"Zimmerman?" he said at last. And then again: "*Zimmerman?*"

"If it's the *same* Zimmerman."

"How can we know?" Itzik said.

"Go ask him," Zeyda said.

"He *can't* ask him," Itzik said. "He promised."

"Promised? Promised who?"

"Our mother."

"*Nu*, what does she think we are, made of lace?"

John only looked at Zeyda.

"I see," Zeyda said. "In that case, why don't you ask the other *Poileshers?*"

"What could they tell me?"

Zeyda looked at John and smiled.

"You might be surprised."

Zelig Botkin had been first.

"Zimmerman?" he said when John questioned him. "Yes, I did hear of a Zimmerman connected with the resistance. But I never thought it was *our* Zimmerman."

Botkin, only a little taller than John, shook his broad white grocer's apron twice and began spraying with a short garden hose the open crates of vegetables tilted upward at them.

"Did you see him?" John asked.

"No, but I heard of it afterward from a Bundist I knew named Bernstein who fled to Lodz after the uprising. Are you sure this is the same Zimmerman I saw just yesterday taking abuse from Karl Hermann at the Farmers' Market?"

"I don't know if it's the same one," said John. "That's why I came to you."

"Are you hungry?" Botkin said suddenly.

"What? No. Look, did this Zimmerman really throw the first fire bomb at the lead tank?"

Botkin released the hose, reached into the crate and withdrew a large red tomato, its red skin wet and shining. He stepped around again and started in the direction of the counter.

"A Molotov cocktail, yes, from a rooftop. I don't know if it was the *first* bomb, or the *lead* tank. But the Zimmerman I heard of did not serve under Anielewicz, at least not directly. He was with what they called a 'wild' group led by Eleazar Frydenzon, who worked with Anielewicz. They were a bunch of crazy Hasidim drawn into the fighting when the Germans assaulted their yeshiva on Nalewki Street. *That* was where the first battle was. Zamenhoff and Mila was further down the road."

Taking a paring knife between thumb and knuckles he sliced twice, quartering the enormous water-beaded tomato, and let go. It opened like a flower, its four broad petals dripping with seeds.

"Who else was on the rooftop?" asked John.

"I don't know. But no one was there long. Stuka dive bombers were dropping incendiary bombs, and the Germans came in with flame throwers. It was hit and run."

"What happened to the rest of the fighters?"

He gave John and Itzik each a wedge and crammed a third into his mouth. John waited until he had swallowed it.

"What happened to the fighters?" he said again.

"*Nu*, eat, eat."

He waited. John took a bite and looked at Botkin.

"They were almost all of them killed," Botkin went on. "Most of the rest were captured. Some hid, a few of them in Lodz. That's how we knew what had happened."

"What about Zimmerman?"

"I don't know."

"And the other Hasidim?"

"Like I said, I wasn't there. You might try Shmuel Mitler.

He spent some time in Warsaw."

"Were you in Lodz the whole war?" Itzik asked.

"No, my people were from Czestochowa. Most of them worked in the factories at Pelcery and Rakow."

"Are any of them left?" John said.

"John," Itzik said.

"No," Botkin said, tearing off a piece of cellophane from a roll hanging over the counter. He began to wrap the fourth wedge of tomato in it.

"How did *you* get through the war?" John said.

Opening the icebox door Botkin placed the wrapped tomato wedge inside on a rack filled with other small cellophane-covered items, row upon row of them, their contents unrecognizable behind the iced-over wrappings.

"I sold food," Botkin said. "Same as now." He looked at Itzik. "There's plenty more."

"He *smuggled* food," Mitler told them when John and Itzik visited him in his garage.

"Little Botkin?" said John. "Botkin was mixed up in…"—he struggled for the word—"*crooked business?*" He did not know how to say it in Yiddish.

Mitler stuck his head out from under the hood of the Hudson Hornet he was working on. The wind from the exhaust fan behind blew his hair out across his brow.

"*Crooket bissniss?*" Mitler asked. "*Vos ret ir epes?*"

"*Genayvishe shtiklech,*" Itzik said.

"Why not?" said Mitler. "Rumkowski, that *bayzeh chaiah*, was selling off Jewish rations to the highest bidder. Most of it made its way to the Aryan side of the city. But there were some who took the trouble to bring it back in."

"Because there was money in it," John said.

"Sure there was money in it. What of it? I had an aunt in Lodz who lived through the war because she was able to get smuggled food. Maybe *Botkin's* smuggled food. Don't be so quick to judge."

"Never mind that," Itzik said. "Ask him about Zimmerman."

"Zimmerman?" Mitler said. "Why should I know about Zimmerman?"

"We hear Zimmerman was in the uprising."

"Go on."

"You didn't know?"

"I don't know anything about it."

"Botkin said you were in Warsaw."

"Not at that time. But I was there the November before that. I jumped a deportation train and made my way back there. You know what a deportation train was?"

Itzik nodded.

"Four days we were in that train, mostly standing still, and thirsty like you can't understand. You know what saved us? At one point some Polish kids came by insulting us and then started heaving snowballs at us through the window grate. Everybody scrambled for the snow. When the kids saw what was what they started charging us money. Soon, money was flying out, snowballs were flying in. Zlotys and snow everywhere."

"Jesus Christ, Mitler," said John.

"Me and a friend, a guy named Reisztayn, we saw someone pry off the window grid and jump out. After a while we followed. One of the Ukrainians saw us from the rooftop of the train and fired, but I knew they weren't going to stop the whole train because of two runaway Jews. I shook my fist at him and yelled, '*Yob tvayu mat!*' You motherfucker!"

John nodded approvingly.

"What did you find in Warsaw?" Itzik asked.

"What I saw, you don't want to know, Walker."

"Tell us," said John.

Mitler removed the float from the carburetor, shook it briskly several times to dry it off, and set it down gingerly on a red rag draped over the wing of the fender.

"All right," he said. "Maybe you should."

He set the float on the radiator cap, wiped his hands on the rag, and replaced both on the fender.

"When I was there, remember, the ghetto was near the end of its days. Everybody who could had gotten out. Everybody who was left had eaten everything that could be eaten already. It was a city full of skeletons. Even the kids. I saw kids, little kids, younger than you even, orphans, walking the streets barefoot and begging for food. And it was freezing. I kept reaching into my pocket for a handkerchief to wipe their noses, and I kept coming up empty. I was using it for an armband. What was the use anyway? In the morning you would always find some frozen from the cold."

"What did you do?"

"I got out, the same way I came—over the wall by the cemetery. It was guarded, but the smugglers had already bribed the guards to look the other way. When they went over, I did too."

"What about your friend?"

"He had family in the ghetto and decided to stay."

"Is he still alive?"

"No," said Mitler. "He had five brothers and sisters. Only one sister is left. She came over here and settled in Crown Heights. Look, haven't you had enough of this? I've got to finish this carburetor before four."

"Not yet," said John. "Where did you go?"

"Where could I go? In the ghetto I found out the name of a woman who could get me some documents. She called herself Wladyslawa Kowalska."

"A *shiksa*?"

"A Jew," said Mitler. "A nice *yiddisher maidel* with a *goyisher* face and a *goyisher* name." He looked carefully at John. "Like *you*, Walker."

"I had a grandfather from a different part of the old country," said John. "His name was O'Day."

"That explains the bricktop," said Mitler.

"Forget that. What did this Kowalska girl do?" John asked.

"Kowalska wasn't her real name. What her name really was I never knew. But she got me my papers, and some money, and I got a job as a mechanic for a little while. But in the end they picked me up."

"How?"

"Some boys came into the shop one day, not much older than you. They said they wanted me to make a donation to their club."

"Who were they?"

"We called them *szmalcownicy*—Polacks who spotted Jews and kept quiet for a little pocket money."

"Did you pay them?"

"You bet I paid them. Then I picked up some tools and left. I still had my documents. I figured I could still find work."

"Did you?"

"I sure did. I got picked up outside of the city by the local police. They sent me to Skarzysko, a labor camp."

"For being a Jew," John added.

"No. I still had my papers. They were all good."

"What for then?"

Mitler sighed, stood back, and looked into his engine; and the Hornet, with its huge center headlight, regarded him in turn. From behind blew the exhaust fan, raising Mitler's hair into a long comb.

"For stealing tools," he said.

"Did she really tell you Zimmerman was there?" Itzik asked.

"She said she knew of a fighter they called Aryeh. That's Zimmerman."

"You didn't really see this woman in Crown Heights, John, did you?"

"Where did you think I was yesterday?"

"You told Abba you were playing baseball."

"Do you want to hear the rest?"

"Go ahead."

"Her brother was in the battle at Nalewki Street. When the Germans came in with the flamethrowers they were trapped on the rooftops. Soldiers were waiting at the bottom of the staircase and their escape route was blocked by the flamethrowers."

"Zimmerman too?"

"Zimmerman was *gone*."

"Gone?"

"They looked around, and no one could see him. Then, a few minutes later, he reappeared behind the Nazis with one of their own flamethrowers."

"How?"

"She couldn't say. But he attacked them all and the Jewish fighters were able to get away."

"He attacked them?"

"He *fried* them."

Itzik shook his head.

"And you said he was just a *luftmensch*."

"A *faiermensch*!" said John.

Itzik closed his eyes. Involuntarily images flashed before him: flames searing and charring a row of rooftops, loud screams filling the air, and Zimmerman, a wayward Prometheus, descending, winding through subterranea, emerging before a lone black-suited figure to battle and plunder and steal back, hurling forth from his hands coarse waves of flame thundering thick-breathed below. Dust reddening. Ashes writhing. Survivors fleeing in loud gutteral bootclumps the annihilating saviour.

Opening his eyes, he said:

"*Zimmerman?*"

"Zimmerman?" Dora Lefkowitz asked. "Are you sure you don't mean Zuckerman? Anielewicz had a right-hand man named Zuckerman with him. They called him Antek."

"You see?" Itzik said. "We're talking about two different people. At *least* two different people."

"No, it was Zimmerman," John said.

"Which Zimmerman? Anielewicz's, or Frydenzon's?"

"It was the same man."

"You mean he was on Zamenhoff and Nalewki at the same time?"

"It wasn't the same time. Mila and Zamenhoff was *afterward.*"

"And you make fun of *me* for believing everything."

"It's not the same."

"And if he *was* at Zamenhoff, was he on the rooftop throwing bombs, or on the street with a flamethrower?"

"Both on the rooftop and on the street."

"Come on, John. How could he get away from a building surrounded on all sides and, let's not forget, burning at the same time?"

"I don't know," John told him.

"Probably by means of a tunnel," Nora Leibgott told them. "*Zhob*—the Jewish Army—had a whole series of tunnels connecting various houses and bunkers in the ghetto. They also used the sewers, which ran everywhere under the city."

"You see?" John told Itzik. "*That's* how he did it. That's how he could reappear on the other side of the street under fire."

"Why did they build tunnels if they could use the sewers?" Itzik asked.

"Because the Germans had maps of the sewers and they could block them, although not for long. *Zhob* lieutenants like Marek Edelman and Aryeh Wilner and Michal Rozenfeld constantly patroled the underground routes and unblocked them."

"How did they see?" Itzik asked.

"They used water lamps, the kind that was used in the ghetto. They were made of two pots. One held chips of calcium carbide, the other water. As the water dripped onto the chips acetylene gas formed, which could be lit as it escaped from the top."

"And von Stroop couldn't stop them?"

"Not easily. He tried flooding them out. That didn't work. Then he had creosote poured in. That didn't work either. Finally he used gas bombs. It made no difference. There were a lot of sewers, and the Nazis couldn't block them all. When the fighting was almost over in the ghetto, several dozen of Anielewicz's soldiers made their way out by way of the sewers. Then they were driven in trucks supplied by the communists to reach the Lowianki Forest. I went there myself after Bialystok fell."

"Did you know Zimmerman was one of them?"

"*Our* Zimmerman?"

"That's right."

"The shammes?"

John nodded.

"I had no idea he was there."

"Do you know where he went afterward?"

"No."

John told her.

"How do you know?"

"How else? I can read."

He told her what he had seen at the wall. "Who do you think would tell me about that?"

Nora pulled out her knitting.

"Nobody," she said.

John waited.

"Ask the Greek," she said at last. "He'll know."

"Who?"

"The Greek. Pesach Anghelakis. He was there."

"How do you know?"

"The same way you know about Zimmerman."

"But how can you be so sure he'll be able to tell us?"

"The Greeks were the smartest and the shrewdest of all of them. Everything that went on there, they knew."

"Where is he?"

"He has a shop by Five Corners, just a couple of blocks up from the Farmers' Market at the Square."

"And he'll know?"

"He'll know."

She looked again at her knitting and began to work. Itzik pulled at John's sleeve, and the two made their way out. But a few minutes later John poked his head back in again.

"Did you say Aryeh *Wilner?*"

It was at this time that Abba found out what John had been doing and brought an end to it. He took John alone with him into the kitchen, closed the door, and spoke with him a long time. When it was over Itzik asked John:

"What did he say?"

"He told me that what he and Ma said about Zimmerman applied to the *Poileshers.* No more questions."

"What are you going to do?"

"The Greek isn't a *Poilesher.*"

"*John.*"

"Just don't say anything."

"When are you going?"

"First chance I get. Maybe this Shabbos. Want to come?"

"No. You know what Abba meant."

"Come on, Itz."

"I said no."

At that moment Abba walked in. John looked at Itzik and left.

By this time John had replaced his map of Ireland on the closet door with one of Warsaw. On it were the same colored tacks, now noting, however, each street skirmish he uncovered in the course of his questioning. That, in the end, was what had fascinated John most: a war in the streets, an army of young Jewish streetfighters. That he could understand. By now he could name the Warsaw streets as readily as he could those in their own neighborhood. He applied himself to memorizing the dates of battles and the names of Warsaw fighters and units with the same care as he had once taken to document the times and terrain of the O'Days. MacManus lay collecting dust beneath the nighttable. Zeyda had been right: John *had* been surprised by the DPs. And they, in turn, in the months that John had taken upon himself the burden of recording their histories, seemed to come to flower. In the synagogue it was noticed, not without interest, that they had begun to sit together, first in pairs, then in larger groups, until at last it was understood that the four rows of benches behind Zimmerman's *bima* were reserved for them.

And today, even as John and Itzik and Abba arrived, they were all of them there. At once they turned to him.

"Deputy *Zhob* commandant," someone fired at him as he walked in.

"Marek Edelman."

From another end:

"Command bunker?"

"Mila 29."

And another:

"April 27?"

"The warehouse fire at Leszno 72. My birthday. You knew that, Botkin."

"*Oi, Gott,* a ringer. All right, what about Niuta Teitelboim?"

"That was Wanda. She blew up the Cafe-Club and robbed the Bank of Poland. Right?"

"Almost, almost," laughed Mitler, putting an arm around him. "How did you know that one?"

"My grandfather."

It was true; John now went often to their grandfather's; they were great friends. For though he did not know it, Aryeh Zimmerman, bricklayer, Racziker Hasid, Zhob fighter, had done that too: brought John and Zeyda together in common worship.

Now came Zimmerman over the *bima*, from the floor of which a long column of light leaned, like a fallen tree, across the synagogue chamber, penetrating the small circular window over the ark. As he passed through it the *bima* darkened suddenly and Zimmerman stood illumined, dustmotes swirling around him like small planets. At the wooden wall he stopped, leaned over the edge, and said:

"Walker, you're late. We're about to start."

"Excuse me, I was held up."

He turned to the boys.

"Nu, Itzik-Betzalel, the day yeshiva principal calls you a scholar. An iron head. A *chacham.*"

"You see, Itzy Bitsy," John said, "you have a reputation."

"About *you,*" Zimmerman went on, "he has little to say."

"How can he? Me, I'm a *chacham bilailah.*"

From all around came shouts and laughter. But Zimmerman only frowned and said:

"What, jokes you're making about the study of Torah? The

613 precepts of law? The history of our holy fathers? The covenant the Oybishter made with Moses and all our people on Sinai? This is not to laugh at, Walker. This is the holy Torah, which Rabbi Akiva compared to the waters of the sea which contain all life. This is the sum of The Name which defines us as what we are."

Zimmerman stopped. After a moment he turned briskly toward the *bima* table. As he did his skullcap flew off to the floor, and Zimmerman, not noticing, moved on with measured strides: once, twice. At the third step John made a great leap, landing with both feet on the wooden wall with a slam that brought Zimmerman to a halt just before he could take the fourth and final step that would complete the transgression. When he turned, John, mouth gaping, pointing to the ground, sang out:

> Litvak, Polack, Zimmerman, nu,
> kimme hir un zog mir, vos bistu?
> Luftmensch, faiermensch, ubermensch, du,
> Zog mir, Reb Zimmerman, vi haistu?

For a moment, the entire synagogue was silent, and everyone stared at John as he stood balanced on the wall, his head even with Zimmerman's. Then John jumped onto the *bima* floor and with great aplomb reached down, scooped up the skullcap, and handed it to Zimmerman with a flourish. At once, there was an explosion of laughter. Chins trembled, eyes streamed, faces furrowed into deep red wrinkles, and as one the entire congregation of *Eytz Chayim* of Paulus Hook rocked back and forth slowly, infants all of them, laughter their cradle. And when old Ephraim Glass dropped weakly into a chair, wheezing and dribbling the while, John handed him a handkerchief which he pulled from his pocket and at once they all remembered his face when he had handed

Zimmerman his *yarmulka* and the laughter redoubled. From the benches, the balconies, the *bima*, the aisles, from all corners came a great sudden unstoppable outpouring of laughter that inundated the synagogue and drowned out utterly all other noise. From the balcony came shrill cries from the women and children, from the aisles the deep bellowing of the big-bellied men. From the back the teenagers hooted and called, and the crowd at the *bima* laughed loudest of all: Zimmerman, Walker, Kravitz, Glass, Plotkin and Botkin and Mitler and Bass, Lefkowicz, Hirschkowitz, Horowitz, Baum, Ostereicher, Westheimer, Steinnoort, Dromm. They laughed, they snorted, they snickered, they giggled. Litvak and Polack, Ashkenazi, Sephard, each man, each woman, each child laughed each without exception each in his own way. Even little Mikhail Szternik, who had no voice, gaped breathlessly as he pounded the top of the *bima* wall with his hand; and he had seen Dachau. And Apfelbaum, beside him, Koldyczewo. And Nussman, just behind, Belzec. And Hirschkowicz, to his left, Belsen. And the rest of the four long terrible rows crowded behind the four wooden walls of Zimmerman's *bima* all joined in as well in the laughter, adding their names too: Treblinka, Majdanek, Gross-Rosen, Ravensbruck, Flossenburg, Buchenwald, Waldheim, Hinzert; Sachsenhausen, Mauthausen, Neuengamme, Nuremburg, Stutthof-Kulmhof, Natzweiler-Struthof, Theresienstadt, Sobibor, Krakow, Mrozy, Siedlce Bedzin Blizyn Vught Lukow Lwow Lodz Ponar Buna Dora Nora Vilna Odessa Czestochowa Zdunska-Wola Rawa-Ruska Poniatowa Chelmno Dubno Kutno Grodno Kovno Opoczno Kopernik Slabodka Babi-Yar Bialisk Kiev Radom Radzymin Raczik Lublin Pinsk Salonika Paris Berlin Amsterdam Danzig Warsaw; Zamosc, Auschwitz; Bialystok, Auschwitz; Roksik, Auschwitz; Krasnystaw, Auschwitz; Auschwitz. Each name named another, named names present even in absence, endless names, countless names, names myriad and luminous and far-flung and hung in the vault of night. It was long laughter, hard laughter, laughter of lung and heart and limb, long, hard-lived laughter. And even Itzik, who normally never laughed, although his name, oddly enough, *meant* laughter, Itzik Isaac Yitzhok Itzik-Betzalel (Itsy-Bitsy) Walker (once Wisniewskiewicz) laughed hysterically along with Horowitz and Apfelbaum and Zimmerman and mute Mikhail Szternik so long and hard he thought his heart would burst; and forgot then that only last week he had, unknown to anyone, climbed the rusted zig-zags of the fire escape attached to the nearby bathhouse building where Zimmerman lived on high, that he had at last, after long deliberation, peered under the drawn shade inside to see, in the dimly lit room, not the pious Racziker Hasid, nor the fierce Frydenzoner soldier, nor even the gentle synagogue shammes, but only a bare back, thick with old welts, rising and falling, and bare legs, almost a child's legs, thinner than he thought thin could be; and for the rest of his life nothing he would ever see or hear or read of the days of what Lichtenbojm had called That Which We Do Not Name would ever equal what he read then in the arcane cicatricial script before him at that moment; and he would have sworn, had he dared to speak, that he would never laugh again.

A sharp blow from behind suddenly sat him down in his seat; and as he rubbed his head gingerly he saw, lying in the aisle beside him, a small round bulging object, its brown skin split and spilling out raisins, nuts, milk-white crystals of sweet rock candy. From all around he now became aware of the sounds of scattered thumps and surprised joyful screams and, looking up, he saw the women raining down from the balcony above the small paper bags Zimmerman had so painstakingly prepared for the day's *ufruf.* Zimmerman himself simply stood on the *bima*, laughing, his arms upraised, his prayer shawl streaming to his feet, the gold-moted column of light falling over him from the window as he stood, taking in the blessings the women bestowed, and smiling joyously. And as Itzik watched Zimmerman, he remembered him by the wall as John had stepped out from behind the corner, smiling broadly, brazenly, his wild red O'Day bricktop flying in the wind, while he held up, for Zimmerman to see, a lean, arched, glistening forefinger still wet with the red of Zimmerman's wall; and Zimmerman, seeing John, had smiled too, that same smile he had now, an enormous beaming lifting smile that broke radiantly across his face, like a rift in the clouds. "A good smile," John had said later, approvingly. "Shows a solid skeleton." It was an amazing smile, a smile, Itzik thought even then, that bespoke miracles. And even as Zimmerman had smiled despite himself he raised his hand to his beard to hide it, and as the open sleeve rolled down to his elbow John and Itzik could see, across the forearm, small, thick blue numbers smeared with age. Only then did they understand Zimmerman's labors, and the great wall, and why, just then, Zimmerman smiled to see one of his own.

Siobhan Dowd of International PEN's Writers-in-Prison Committee in London writes this column regularly, alerting readers to the plight of writers around the world who deserve our awareness and our writing action.

Silenced Voice: Carlos Cardoso
by Siobhan Dowd

Carlos Cardoso

*M*ozambique has enjoyed independence from Portugal for only twenty-five years; the first seventeen of those were blighted by civil war. This poor and flood-stricken southern African country has struggled to throw off its unhappy past, but despite a thriving intellectual community in the capital, Maputo, and improved relations with its influential neighbor, South Africa, a happier chapter is yet to open. This fact was underscored by the recent assassination of Carlos Cardoso, one of Mozambique's most colorful figures in the media.

Cardoso was an old-fashioned Marxist at heart, and broadly

Glimmer Train Stories, Issue 40, Fall 2001
© 2001 Siobhan Dowd

sympathetic to the ruling Frelimo regime; but this did not prevent him, over a long journalistic career, from directing sharp criticisms at the government's more corrupt aspects, and this always meant he was vulnerable to attack. Recently he said that he felt safe, as he had survived so long without suffering the consequences of his outspokenness. But he obviously spoke too soon: his brutal killing by unknown assailants on November 22, 2000, was proof, if proof were needed, that his warnings and criticisms were only too germane.

He is much mourned at home and abroad. The world's major newspapers have carried obituaries, and in Maputo the prime minister has lamented him as a vigorous voice for a free press, promising to leave no stone unturned in bringing his killers to justice. This may prove difficult and politically delicate—for there is every reason to believe that government elements themselves may have been involved.

Cardoso was born in 1952 in the town of Beira in the heart of Mozambique. His father, a dairy-factory manager, sent him to neighboring South Africa for a secondary and tertiary education. Here he launched himself into leftist politics while a student at the University of Witwatersrand in Johannesburg; after the 1974 coup in Portugal he is said to have unfurled the Frelimo flag on the campus. A year later, Mozambique became independent. Cardoso's father was among the many Portuguese who quit the country—more or less as Cardoso returned, having been deported from apartheid South Africa because of his Marxist views.

He immediately found work at *Tempo*, a pro-government newspaper, but soon began to irritate his political bosses—to such an extent that he was in effect demoted to Radio Mozambique's music department. But by 1980, he was back in favor and appointed as editor of the AIM, a government press agency, where he remained for nine years. During this time, he was once jailed for nearly a week for a story he wrote about the rebel movement, Renamo; the then president Samora Machel (who was himself later assassinated) is said to have taken personal exception to it, but whatever breach there was seems to have been healed, for, soon afterwards, Cardoso became one of Machel's key advisors. He is said to have warned Machel of danger, and afterwards, he investigated Machel's death, claiming that though he had been murdered in South Africa, the killers were strongly linked to Mozambique.

Cardoso then went through a period of disenchantment. He withdrew from his prominent place in the media and turned to painting. Nevertheless he added his weight to a campaign for greater press freedom, and this led in 1991 to the passage of a new and relatively liberal (given its African context) press law. Encouraged by this, he rejoined the fray, but this time as an independent: he co-founded Mediafax, where he worked until 1997, and then set up Metical. These two news bureaus operated on a system of faxed news sheets to subscribers. Both became essential reading in Mozambique, for they were briskly efficient, impartial, and probing, and followed far higher standards of investigative reporting than any of their conventional equivalents. Cardoso, as editor, oversaw such stories as one lambasting the World Bank for its suppression of Mozambique's cashew-nut processing industry, and another revealing how Mozambique's source of illegal income came from its being an international drug thoroughfare. (His own stance on drugs was apparently for the legalization of at least marijuana: his friend Joseph Hanlon, in his obituary in the London *Guardian*, recalls that one of his more madcap ideas had been to turn "marijuana into a major export crop.")

Just before his killing he had been probing the Banco Commercial de Moçambique: Metical claimed that a cool twelve million dollars had been siphoned off during the process of the bank being sold off. He turned a spotlight on the Attorney-General's office and said that "gangster elements" within the ruling party itself ought to be prosecuted. In 1999, a lawyer for the bank, Albano Silva, narrowly escaped murder in an ambush that was strikingly similar to what was awaiting Cardoso.

The day he died, Cardoso was being driven through the center of town, close to his office, when two vehicles drew level, cutting him off. At least two men are said to have got out and opened fire at point-blank range with AK-47 assault rifles. His driver was seriously wounded; Cardoso was killed outright. A TV crew arrived on the scene soon afterwards and immediately broadcast what it found: the whole of Mozambique watched, appalled, as his bullet-ridden body was removed from the car.

Hilario Matusse, the Mozambican Journalists' Union's general secretary, mourned his loss as a blow to the country's newfound press freedom. "Carlos Cardoso," he said, "was a person who always spoke his mind. But if anyone disagreed with him, he was always willing to sit down and discuss it with him." The Prime Minister Pascoal Mocumbi said he was "deeply shocked" and "profoundly affected" by Cardoso's death. "He was a journalist who always fought tirelessly for freedom of the press," he added. Cardoso is survived by his Norwegian wife Nina and their son and daughter.

Please write letters asking the Mozambique government to investigate fully Cardoso's murder, and to bring its perpetrators—whoever they might be—to justice, to:

His Excellency Joaquím Chissanó
President of Mozambique
c/o H.E. High Commissioner to United Kingdom
London, UK
Fax: 011 44 207 7383 3801

Tom Kealey

Although they would probably deny it today, my parents used to stick me in this milkbox in the mornings, in the hope that the milkman would come along and take me away. This was the 1970s, though, and I guess there hadn't been milk delivery on Long Island for about forty or fifty years. After this, they tried to stuff me into the mailbox, but I wouldn't fit.

Tom Kealey is a student in the creative-writing department at the University of Massachusetts. He also teaches College Writing to a group of eighteen and nineteen year olds who continually surprise him (pleasantly) with their creativity, intelligence, and humor.

Tom says he misses his friends in the great state of North Carolina, especially Eric and Ashly, who keep a few cold beers in the refrigerator for his next trip home. He'd also like to say hi to Michael, Cathy, Meena, Tommy, Kelcie, Steadman, Alyssa, Jerry, Abby, Jen, Nancy, Kate, David, Kristy, Allison, Matt, Chris, Jeff, and Dawn, most of whom he called and said, "Yee-haw! I got into *Glimmer Train*!"

Finally, since "Groundskeeping" is a story with some heart, he'd like to dedicate it to his parents and sister. Here's to you.

TOM KEALEY
Groundskeeping

*I*t was the day after my fourteenth birthday, and I'd been looking out the window of the bus for most of Tennessee and into the Appalachians, watching the fog rise from the shoulder of the road and the patchwork of barns and homes near the state highway. A pale, spotted horse here, a brown dog lying on its side there, a group of young girls, about my age, dancing to music from a tape player set on the hood of a car. When we pulled into the station I spotted my Uncle Jake, dressed in a blue T-shirt and jeans, leaning against one of the support poles. I recognized the wide green eyes from a picture my dad kept on our mantel at home. In the picture, my dad is propped on the trunk of a yellowing Ford Pinto, a serious, solemn look on his face, even as a boy, the dark curly hair, like mine, falling down his temples—and Jake, leaning back on the fender of the car, a slight, wild grin curving from his lips, a cigarette dangling from his fingers at age fifteen. The bus driver swung open the door and called out, "Morganton. Five-minute stop," but even as I stepped across the legs of the man sitting next to me, I noticed I was the only one getting off.

Glimmer Train Stories, Issue 40, Fall 2001
©*2001 Tom Kealey*

I stepped down onto the platform and felt the smack of the July sun on my face. Jake ambled over and reached for the small duffel bag in my hand, but I said, "I got it."

"Is that all you got?"

"That's all I got," I said.

"Well, all right then," said Jake.

His transportation was a blue flatbed pickup truck, rusted on the fenders, with a dent in the passenger-side door. In the cab I was introduced to Mulligan, a sandy-colored, over-weight mutt with four white paws, like boots. Mulligan scooted to the middle of the seat and sniffed at my duffel bag.

"He's got a tick in his ear," I said to Jake as I closed the door. "It's been there for a few days."

"Is that right?" he said, turning the key, but no sound came from the motor. He reached under the seat and pulled out a long-stem hammer, popped the hood, and got back out of the truck.

While he was banging on the starter in the engine I took out the tweezers from my pocket knife and picked up the book of matches lying on the dashboard. I lit one, letting it burn for a moment. Mulligan sniffed at the sulfur in the air. When I blew the match out I stuck it quickly to the tick, yellow and fat, its legs shuddering as I grabbed hold of Mulligan's orange collar and said, "Take it easy." I clamped the tweezers shut near the head of the tick, squeezing and prying it loose as quick as I could, and then tossing it out the window with the match. Mulligan glanced sideways at me, wrinkling the white stripe of fur that ran down his snout.

When the motor turned over, Jake backed out onto a two-lane road and ran his fingers along the dashboard, eventually giving up and punching the cigarette lighter on the console. "How was the trip?" he asked.

"Long. Boring," I said.

"Did you read your books?"

"I did."

"I hear you're a big reader."

"You heard right."

"What'd you read?"

"A book about mountain climbing and a book about sharks."

"Are you a mountain climber?"

"No."

"I caught a shark on the Outer Banks last summer," he said. "Hooked him with a spring rod. Three and a half feet. A mako." The cigarette lighter popped out and Jake lit up without taking his eyes off the road.

"Makos aren't found on the Outer Banks. They're only found in warm climates."

"This was summertime," he said.

"Summer isn't warm enough. It was probably a nurse shark. They're harmless and are an endangered species."

"A nurse shark, you say?"

"That's right."

"How do you know?"

"When we get to the house I'll take a look."

"What makes you think I've got it at the house?" he said.

Mulligan leaned against me as we took a turn. I looked over at Jake. "You seem like the kind of guy who would have the one shark he ever caught stuffed and put up over his mantel."

"I don't have a mantel," said Jake.

"Do you have a stuffed shark on the wall?"

"Yes, I do."

"It's a nurse shark."

"You want to bet?"

"No," I said.

"You afraid of losing?"

"No, I don't bet, that's all."

"A betting man is a man who knows what he's talking about," he said. "You sound like you know what you're talking about. Why don't you take the bet?"

I looked over at him. "My dad said you once lost a house in a poker game."

Jake puffed off his cigarette and flicked the ashes out the window. "He did, did he?"

"Yes, he did."

"Well," he said. "You shouldn't believe everything you hear."

"My dad wasn't a liar."

"I didn't say he was."

"Yes, you did. You just said it."

"When did I say it?"

"You inferred it."

"Oh," said Jake. "I inferred it."

The truck was in need of new shocks and bounced in the road at every slight pothole and bump. We drifted down an off ramp and onto a state highway, still two lanes.

"Your dad was a good man," said Jake. "But he and I were not that close."

I didn't say anything.

"How long you staying?"

"Until I hear from my mom."

"How long's that going to be?" he said.

"Not long."

Jake rubbed his hand along the wheel. "Well, I've got some rules that I want you to know about."

"You do?"

"Yes," he said. "I do."

On the highway we passed the Bond's Motel, a long brown building with an empty swimming pool. Stands with signs for homemade honey and fresh vegetables appeared every quarter mile or so, and a brick building advertising violin repair.

Mulligan sat down on his haunches, licked his paw, and rubbed at the ear where the tick had been.

I asked Jake if he was going to tell me what these rules were. I told him my psychic powers weren't too good.

"Your dad was a smart ass, too," said Jake.

"Better than being a dumb ass," I said.

Jake laughed, his white-stubbled jaw reaching forward as he blew smoke out his mouth. "I taught him that one," he said. "Better than being a dumb ass."

"You must be real proud," I said.

"Rule one," said Jake. "I watch a lot of TV. If you don't like what I'm watching, then too bad. In my house, I'm in charge of the remote."

"I don't watch TV," I said.

"Well, I guess that won't be a problem."

"Guess not."

"Well, all right, then," he said.

"Okay, then," I said.

"Rule two," he said. "I need my sleep. I've got to be at the ballpark at 8 A.M., so no making loud noises in the middle of the night."

"I don't make loud noises in the middle of the night."

"Well, I guess it won't be a problem."

"I guess not."

"Rule three," he said. "If you break something, you pay for it."

I asked him if he was running an antique shop.

"No, I'm just saying. Don't go breaking my things."

"I won't."

"Rule four," he said, rubbing his hands back and forth along the steering wheel. He flicked the ashes from his cigarette out the window again. Outside on the road we passed a veterinarian clinic and a stretch of farmland, silos and grey barns cluttered together. Jake leaned back in the seat and glanced over at me. "Well," he said. "I can't think of anything. I guess there is no number four."

"I've got some rules, too," I said.

"You do?"

"I do."

"Well, let's hear them."

"First," I said. "You want to smoke, then that's your preroga-tive, but there's the issue of secondary smoke. I don't want you bringing your cigarettes into my room, and I want the door to my room closed, and I want it kept closed."

"Who says you're getting a room?" he said.

"I just got off a thirty-six-hour bus ride. I better have a room."

Jake turned the wheel at exit 20 and gunned the engine up the on ramp. Outside, the clouds had covered the sun.

"Did you know," I said, "a smoker can quit after seven years, and in seven more years he can have lungs that are as healthy as a person who's never smoked."

"Is that a fact?"

"I read it," I said. "It doesn't make it a fact. There are some exceptions, but for most people, that's the case."

"I see."

"How long have you smoked for?"

"Thirty-three years."

I rolled down the window to get at some air. "You're screwed," I said. "That makes you at least forty-eight years old."

"How do you figure?"

"Am I right?"

"I'll be fifty this December."

"If you make it to December," I said.

"Uh-huh," he said, and flicked ashes out the window.

"Second," I said. "I don't have much stuff, but what I have I don't want you looking through. I've got a letter from my dad to you. I'll give you that when we get home."

"What's it say?"

"I don't know," I said. "He told me if anything ever happened to him I was supposed to give it to you."

"And you never looked at it?"

"No," I said. "It wasn't for me, it's for you."

"What do you have that you don't want me to look at?"

"Nothing," I said. "What I've got is mostly clothes and books."

"I don't read too much."

"Then I guess it won't be a problem."

"I guess not," he said.

"Well, all right, then."

"Okay, then," he said. "You got any more rules?"

The cab of the truck bounced as we hit a pothole, and Mulligan placed his paw on my leg. "Not that I can think of," I said. "But I may come up with some more later."

"Me, too," Jake said. "I may come up with some more later, too."

We turned onto a gravel driveway, covered overtop with the arching limbs of pine trees. The truck continued to bounce and lean as we made our way to the house, a wooden A-frame with a chimney, blackened at the top, and a railless porch on the second story. Mulligan wagged his tail and turned to look at Jake.

"This is home," Jake said.

"If you say so," I said.

The spotlights in Memorial Stadium can be seen just over the treetops on highway 64, right next to the scoreboard with the big sign for Coca-Cola. When I arrived in mid-season, the Morganton Knights were eleven and a half games out of first place in the South Atlantic League and not looking to move up any time soon. I'll say this for Jake: he kept a good field. The grass in the outfield was a bright green, and he kept the baselines razor straight, not allowing the dirt to form a lip into the infield diamond. Somehow he conned some local kids into dragging the baselines with rakes in the middle of the fifth inning, and on the nights when it rained—which was often—the Knights players themselves helped pull the light-blue tarp over the dirt on the pitcher's mound and around the bases.

I got ten dollars to mow the outfield three times a week, alternating between the 305 (the distance between the foul poles) and the checkerboard cut, plus another two bucks to make sure the lime was dropped on the baselines before each game.

The second week I was there, the team mascot—some teenager dressed up in a suit of armor, no joke—passed out from heat exhaustion during the seventh-inning stretch. We could hear him clatter to the ground next to the concession stand, like a tray of china dropped on the floor. After the games, Jake and I dragged the infield again and he ran his hands through the grass, testing for soft spots. The night before a homestretch against the Gastonia Cougars, he flipped the floodlights off in the stadium and carried a lantern and a shovel in a wheelbarrow out to first base. I knelt with him in the dirt.

"The Cougars've got this kid named Ellis," he said. "He's stolen everything this year except the catcher's underwear, but we're going to fix him good."

He pitched the shovel into the ground and removed the topsoil where a runner would take a lead off first base. Down in its place he scooped a mix of peat moss, water, and sand. Then he covered the mixture with a thin layer of the topsoil, slapping it flat with the back of the shovel. "When your man digs his cleats in here, he's gonna sink like the *Lusitania*."

"Is this legal?" I asked.

"If no one finds out about it."

"It's cheating," I said.

"Well," said Jake. "You could call it that. You could also call it 'home-field advantage.'" For good measure he slanted the baselines around homeplate so that any bunted ball would curve straight to the pitcher.

Some nights we took turns hitting soft loopers into the outfield, with Mulligan running out into the dark to retrieve them.

"You're not a bad hitter," said Jake after I slapped the ball, off a bounce, against the yellow and blue sign for Denny's in left field. That was weeks later, after he'd shown me how to stand in the batter's box and dig my right foot into the dirt. "Choke up on the bat," he said. "When you get older and your arms bulk up you can grab it at the bottom. There's no shame in doing what works. You're not going to be Hank Aaron in two weeks."

"Who's Hank Aaron?" I said, but I knew.

"Jesus," said Jake, and pitched a fastball smack over home plate.

When it was his turn to bat he could smack the ball into either corner of the field—triple territory—and a few times he'd knock it over the wall, something I think he would've done more often if we'd had more baseballs with us.

If it was late enough at night, after we collected the equipment and put it away in the shed, and after Jake walked the field one last time, plugging holes in the batter's box and pitcher's mound with wet clay from a tin bucket, he'd push the driver's seat in the pickup truck forward and let me drive home. We never saw a police car on the back roads. Most nights I had to smack the starter with the hammer two or three times to get the engine to turn over, and then I'd push in the clutch gently and back out of the lot.

"Did you get the emergency brake?" said Jake.

"I did."

"I didn't see you do it."

"You weren't watching close enough."

The breeze slanting through the windows was cold at night, even into late July, and I kept the speedometer needle steady at forty or forty-five. After a time or two, Jake leaned back in the passenger seat and pushed his baseball cap over his eyes, Mulligan leaning across him with his head out the window. Every few minutes Jake stretched his legs out in the cab and I could hear the *pop-pop* of his kneecaps and hear him sigh in relief.

"Your mom's got my number?" said Jake.

"She does."

"You told her you were staying here?"

"I didn't talk to her," I said. "I told her neighbor on the phone, and he said he'd give her the message."

"Your mom still in that hospital?"

"What do you know about it?"

"I don't know anything except what your dad told me in the letter."

"What'd he say in the letter?"

He flipped the cap up over his eyes and looked out the windshield. "The turn's coming up here."

"I know where it is."

"Why haven't you asked me about the letter before now?"

"Because," I said, "the letter was for you. I try to stay out of people's business."

Jake nodded. "That you do."

"You don't have to tell me if you don't want to."

"I'll tell you."

I glanced over at him. "Well, what are you waiting for then?"

He looked out on the road. "I'm waiting for you to make this turn up here that we're going too fast to make."

I pressed down on the brake and made the turn. A sedan in the other lane stopped and the driver shook his head as I swerved over the line. The trees overhead began to block out the stars.

"Your dad said that your mom's been in and out of Frank Wood Hospital in Phoenix, which is a mental hospital, and she may not be able to take care of you."

I didn't say anything. Mulligan stuck his head back in from the window and tried to lean across my lap. I pushed him away.

"He said you were something special," said Jake. "Real smart. Said you skipped the third grade when you were younger."

"I did," I said.

"He said you had a garden back home. Used to raise vegetables."

"I did."

"He said you'd be some help at the ballpark."

"I think I have been."

"Yeah," said Jake, lighting up a cigarette. "You've been all right."

I saw something come out of the woods. I slowed the truck down, and a small deer galloped across the road. His legs flew through the headlights in an instant. We watched him as he disappeared into the woods on the other side of the road, and I punched the clutch again.

"He told me some things about you, too," I said.

"He did, did he?"

"He did."

"Like what?"

"He said you'd drink all day if you could."

Jake blew smoke out the window and propped his foot up against the dashboard. "Not anymore I wouldn't."

"He said you don't speak to your wife or kids anymore."

"Is that a fact?"

"You tell me," I said. "It's just something I heard."

Jake was quiet for a while. The sharp smell of pine drifted into the cab as we approached the driveway. Leaves and dust scattered across the road with the wind.

"Your dad was a harsh man," said Jake.

I nodded. "He could be."

"He never thought I was much help to him growing up."

"Well," I said. "What help were you?"

When we came up to the house I parked the truck next to the vegetable garden, long abandoned, the grass pushing over the soil. On the house, one of the gutters leaned crooked off the roof. I switched off the motor and sat still. Jake opened the door and let Mulligan out, but didn't rise from the cab. We could hear crickets out in the woods, bleating back and forth to each other.

"I don't know, Grady," Jake finally said. "I guess I was never good for much."

Jake didn't watch as much TV as he claimed, and some nights, after we got back from the ballpark, we sat in beach chairs on the second-story roof and looked at the stars. It was cold late in the evening and sometimes I'd throw a thick blanket over my legs. Jake sat next to me and dropped the ashes from his cigarettes into a can filled with topsoil. I learned that when you look straight up around midnight in late summer you can spot Vega, a blue-white star that shines bright in a cluster of other, duller stars in the constellation of Lyra.

"Most constellations don't look anything like they're supposed to," said Jake. "Cassiopeia is supposed to be some lady sitting on a chair, but it looks more like the letter *W*, and Sagittarius is the archer, but he looks just like a teapot. See that orange star just south of Vega?"

"No."

"Right there," he said, pointing with the end of his cigarette. "Right below Vega. It's the beginning of Scorpius, which
actually does look like it's supposed to. That arc there is the
claws of the scorpion, and that hook of stars just underneath
it is the tail."

"If you say so."

"I do."

"How do you know so much about this?"

He leaned forward in the chair and glanced down into the
yard. A pair of groundhogs stood in the yard, silhouetted from
the light in the stars. One of them bent down and dug into
the grass, his front paws working like shovels. We watched
them in silence for a while, until Jake got caught up in a
coughing fit, and the groundhogs stood listening, still as
stumps of trees, and then meandered slowly into the woods.
We were up high enough to see over the treetops, and up on
the horizon I could see Jupiter appear, the first planet Jake
had pointed out to me the week before.

"How do you know so much about the sky?" I asked again.

"Me and my kids used to sit up here. They learned about it
at some class they took at the community center."

"How old are your boys?"

"The oldest will be eighteen this year, and the younger
one's a couple years older than you."

"Where do they live?"

"I'm not sure."

"Don't you ever call them?"

He took a drag off his cigarette. "There's not much point."

I picked up the binoculars from the porch and put them to
my eyes. The moon that night was almost full, and it blocked
out our view of a lot of the constellations. I squinted as I looked
through the lenses, and then when my eyes began to adjust I
could make out the giant crater on the south end of the moon,
with the lunar Alps stretching out in grey and black. There was

a strong breeze that night, the smell of burned wood drifting from the brush fire of one of Jake's neighbors.

"You must be proud of your little stunt tonight," I said.

"Oh," he said. "That's just part of the job."

"I bet," I said. "I bet that's not in the job description."

With two outs in the fourth inning, Gastonia finally got a man on base. When he took a lead off first, digging his heels into the baseline, he sunk about an inch and a half into the dirt. He tried to steal second anyway and got nailed by the catcher with a few steps to spare. The runner walked back to first and swiped his foot at the line, kicking up enough peat moss to have the umpire come out and have a look. The home crowd booed and jeered at him. After a huddle with both managers, the umpire ordered the hole to be filled in, so Jake went out with the wheelbarrow, containing mostly the same mix we'd put in the night before, and filled it over top. Because the baseline then had a mound of sand and muck sticking up on the line, the umpire had Jake water it down, and Jake looped the hose out onto the field and sprayed it over. It all resulted in a kind of overgrown swamp area near first base.

"I think I saw a few fish flopping around out there," I said.

"Yeah," said Jake. "We'll see if we can't catch us one or two tomorrow night."

The mailbox sat at the end of the gravel driveway, and every night when we returned from the ballpark Jake walked down the road with Mulligan, returning a few minutes later, sticking his head into my room. "Nothing came," he said.

"Okay."

My room had a banner for the Atlanta Braves and a chart of the stars on the ceiling that I began to study. A few clothes, about my size, hung on the rack in the closet—a red shirt with pineapple designs on the front, a black pair of corduroys, and two thick, winter jackets with fur lining.

I placed my books on a shelf above one of the desks and slipped my clothes into the top drawer of the dresser. I didn't spend much time in the room because Jake and I were at the ballpark five, sometimes six days out of the week. We arrived at nine or so, after stopping at a diner on the highway for coffee and french toast. If there was a game that night then we stayed at least until eleven o'clock, eating dinner in foil wrappers and styrofoam drink cups. I became pretty good at spotting sunken divots and soft spots in the outfield that we filled with dirt and soil, and the holes in the batter's box and pitcher's mound were packed in with clay.

During the games I could sit in the dugout with the team if I wanted to, but I didn't want to. The players were the kind of men who held spitting contests while the sides were changing, and they told dumb stories about high school— usually involving narrow escapes from the police and strange encounters with women from New York in the backseats of their cars. Mulligan wore a black-and-red kerchief around his neck during home stretches, and he sat in the stands with me, raising his ears at the sound of a ball struck hard or a child screaming in the family section near right field. Mostly, I just read during the games.

I found a lot of books on vegetable gardening in the town library. The soil in the foothills of North Carolina is best for tobacco, but a few food crops grow well, particularly potatoes and soy beans, and by the end of July I'd pulled the weeds and overgrown grass out from the small garden at Jake's house. On our day or two off I began to plant a few rows of onions, carrots, and some other winter vegetables.

One day Jake walked out and stood over me as I knelt in the dirt. "What'd you do to my shovel?"

"What do you mean?"

He picked it up off the ground and fingered the blade. "You cut holes in it."

"I made a serrated edge so I could cut back the weeds. I didn't see a hoe anywhere."

"What'd you cut the holes with?"

"The file in your toolbox."

"Did you blunt it?"

I looked up at him. "What do you mean did I blunt it? Of course I blunted it, that's what it's there for."

"I was going to use that."

"I bet."

"What kind of seeds are those?" he said.

"Leek."

"What's that?"

"It's like an onion."

He stuck the shovel into the dirt. "Nothing's going to come up here. Winter's going to start in two months."

"They'll be up about then."

"Nothing's grown here for a while," he said.

"That's because you haven't planted anything."

"You sure they're going to be up before winter?"

"No."

"Then why are you doing it?"

I stuck the trowel into the ground and scooped up the soil I'd put down the week before. I'd had to dig up the rocks and tree roots and just then was placing seeds in the ground.

"Because if nothing comes up this year, then something will come up next year. You've got to make the ground think like a garden."

"Where'd you learn that?"

"In a book," I said. "They're these thick things with words in them. I'll show you one sometime."

He just stood there, so after a while I put him to work digging five-inch-deep pockets along the left side of the garden. He stuck the shovel into the ground with his boot and chucked the dirt onto the grass.

"Could you keep that in a pile, please?" I said. "We'll need it to fill in the holes."

He didn't say anything, but he scooped it into something resembling a pile.

"And could you try to keep them in a straight line?" I said.

"What's it matter if it's in a straight line?"

"It matters to me."

"So?"

"So," I said. "This is my garden. I'm in charge of it. You're in charge of the baseball field and I'm your assistant there. If you want to help out here, then you're my assistant."

"What are you paying?"

"Nothing," I said.

"Nothing?" he said. "What's the matter, you saving your money for something?"

I dropped bulbs into the holes that he made and covered them up with dirt. I eyed the garden hose, hanging on a nail on the side of the house. At the bottom of the hose were long holes, worn away over time.

"Grady?"

"Yeah?"

"You saving your money for something?"

"Maybe."

"Like what?"

"Nothing."

He shoveled another hole and flipped the dirt onto the growing pile. Looking up, he paused for a moment and said, "It's going to be a good night for watching the stars. Those clouds are moving out."

I packed the dirt down flat on top of the seeds and then wondered why I did that. They needed loose soil so the plant could reach through. I stuck the trowel into the ground and turned it back and forth.

"If you say so," I said.

That Sunday night Jake took an old white sheet out from the closet and pinned it up over the fireplace in the den. From the basement he brought up a large, grey film projector and sat on the couch, threading a line of film into the feeder. Mulligan stretched out on his belly on the thick rug and kept an eye on the ice cream that I'd filled in two bowls. When Jake was finished, he flipped off the lights and turned the projector to the wall. Backwards letters and dark lines, like hair, shot across the screen, and then numbers counted down from seven to two.

Two shapes in the water, out of focus, splashed and kicked at each other until the camera moved closer, and I spotted the dark-haired head of my father as he waved to shore. The film was grainy and yellowed, and everything was in fast motion, like time itself moved faster back then. When they came out of the water, Jake was by far the taller of the two, broad shouldered and wiry. He lay face down on a picnic table and pretended to swim through the air, laughing like an idiot. My father stood behind him a little ways, washing the water out of his ear with a towel, his body skinny enough that I could count his ribs and collarbones.

"That place was called Holden's Creek," said Jake, licking at the ice cream on his spoon. "It was about a half-mile away from the neighborhood we grew up in. Your dad was there all the time. He was a damn good swimmer."

"Who's behind the camera?"

"I don't know. Mom died when your father was about ten, and he looks older than that here."

"Was it your father?"

"No," said Jake. "It wouldn't have been him."

A dog trotted into the picture, a long-haired collie mix, and Jake picked it up by the front paws and began to dance. Behind them, the long leaves of a willow tree leaned forward with the breeze. My father sat on the picnic table, already pulling his shirt over his head and cleaning the dirt from between his toes. He glanced at Jake and the dog for a moment and then rolled his eyes.

"I bet your dad's about thirteen there. He moved away, you know, probably the next year. He lived in Seattle with our grandmother, our mom's mom, and then he went straight into the Coast Guard from there."

"What'd you do?"

"Oh, I just hung around home. They used to have a race track up near where we lived, and I always had the idea that I'd buy a stock car and get onto the circuit, but that never panned out."

"And then you got married?"

"No. I didn't get married for a while. I moved around a bit, taking a job here and there. I worked a lot of construction jobs. They were always easy to find in those days, probably still are. I met my wife in New Mexico, of all places."

"My mom's from New Mexico."

"Is she?" Jake said. "I didn't know that. Lots of good people come from that place."

"My mom knew the stars pretty well," I said. "She used to tell me that it was hard to sleep outside in New Mexico, because the sky was so bright it'd keep you awake."

"Yeah, I suppose that's true. I don't remember, though, I wasn't much for looking up in those days."

"I'd like to see New Mexico."

Jake set his bowl down on the floor for Mulligan. "You probably will. You've got your whole life ahead of you."

The film split to Jake and my dad in the backyard of a house, a wire fence standing crooked behind them. They both wore small, tight boxer's gloves. Jake hopped from toe to toe, bare-chested, tapping my dad on the forehead and then leaping away. Dad kept his head low, sweat spots staining the arms of his T-shirt, stalking Jake slowly, not wasting punches until he was close enough. Jake talked to the camera, but there was no sound, and he stopped every once in a while to wind up his arm as if he was going to throw a wide hook, but Dad kept his gloves up and Jake backed off again.

By the middle of August the Knights crept to within eight games of first place, but then they floundered in a weekend road trip to be eliminated from playoff contention. On our days off I worked at the weeds in the garden, sometimes at night under a full moon, and Jake brought home two buckets from the ballpark so we could water the vegetables in the evenings. The phone never rang in the house. I picked the receiver up from the cradle every few days or so, just to make sure the dial tone was still there.

During the late innings of games Jake sat in the stands with me and Mulligan, and if there was some kind of action down on the field, he'd point or nod his head at a baserunner or an infielder.

"See that shortstop? He's checking the distance between him and second base because of the runner at first. And the third baseman, he's got to cover the gap. If that batter's any good, he can knock a line drive over the bag at third and score the runner."

In between innings I pointed out things in my books, like the picture of the mako shark. "Indigenous to southern climates only," I said.

Jake squinted and looked at the book. "You don't say."

"It does."

On the day before the final home stand, Jake had me cut the outfield extra low near the foul lines, hoping to turn some of the team's doubles into triples, and long after the sunset, he brought a shovel and a pail of dirt out to the pitcher's mound. He put his foot to the blade and dug out a concave shape into the front of the mound, where the pitcher's foot might land.

"What are you doing?" I asked.

He scooped the dirt into the wheelbarrow. "Scouting report on Burlington says they got this new kid. One hell of a fastball. Keeps it low and outside. The Knights can't hit lowballs, never could."

"So?"

"So, when this kid goes into his windup, his foot's going to hit the dirt about a quarter second later than he thought it would, and that ball's going to float up over the plate like a giant piñata."

I stood with my hands in my pockets. "How many games do you think you've won for the Knights this year?"

"Oh," he said, "About seven or eight. Not nearly enough."

I knelt down and packed the dirt down with my hand, smoothing it over so it would be hard to spot by the umpire.

Jake picked up a baseball and threw it into the outfield, and Mulligan jumped up from one of the on-deck circles and chased after it.

"What do you do in the off season, Jake?"

He shrugged. "I work a little in town at a hardware store that an old friend of mine owns, and I still come out to the field every once in a while. Make sure that nobody's messed with it. I'll be pretty busy all the way up to October—going to lay down some new sod in the outfield this autumn, before it gets too cold."

"Sounds like a lot of work."

"Probably will be," he said.

I looked up at him. "I'll probably be gone in a few days," I said. "I'm sorry I won't be around to help you."

He looked at me. "Is that a fact? You hear something from your mom?"

"No. But she'll be ready to take me by the end of the month."

"How do you figure?"

I looked out at the highway past the stadium. A tractor trailer made its way up the hill, and smaller cars passed it on the outside. "It's just what we'd talked about," I said.

"When did you talk to her?"

"Before I came out here."

"Oh," he said. He put the shovel over his shoulder. "I don't remember you mentioning that."

"Maybe I didn't."

"Is she going to send for you?"

"Doesn't matter," I said. "I've almost got enough money to get a bus ride there."

"I see." He placed the rest of the tools into the wheelbarrow. "How much you short?"

"About thirty dollars."

He picked up the wheelbarrow and began to walk toward the shed. "I bet you I can spot you that if you're still short."

I followed behind him. "I'll pay you back."

"No. We'll just call it an end-of-the-season bonus."

"If you say so."

"I do."

We put the tools away in the shed and snapped the lock shut. The truck was parked outside in the space closest to the gate. Jake said he'd drive that night, so I opened the passenger door for Mulligan and then climbed in. Up in the sky, the moon was absent, and I could spot Vega just to the north of center, bright as I'd seen it. We pulled out onto the highway.

"I'll miss having you around," said Jake. "You've been a lot of help to me."

"I'll write you a letter when I get there."

"Do that."

I played with a strip of fabric hanging off the seat cover. "Are you going to write me back?"

"I suppose so."

"I'd like to hear how the garden turns out," I said. I rolled up the window. "Are you going to keep working at it?"

"If you want me to."

"I do."

"All right then," he said.

The road was empty on the ride back. We didn't pass a single car on the state highway or the narrow road leading to the house. When we pulled onto the driveway, the trees covered up the stars and the headlights glowed, shining on the leaves and the tree branches fallen to the ground.

"Thanks for showing me the stars," I said. "I learned a lot while I was here."

"Glad to hear it."

"I'll probably show my mom some of them."

"I'm sure she'd like that," Jake said. He began to roll up his window. "Tell you what. You remember which one Scorpius was?"

"Yep."

"And what's its main star?"

"Antares."

"Okay," he said. "Scorpio's going to rise in the sky as autumn comes, and on into winter. You be sure to look up at Antares every once in a while. Around midnight or so, and I'll be sitting here looking up at it, and that way we'll both be looking at the same thing."

"That sounds good," I said.

"All right then."

When we came out from the treeline, we could see two small shadows stand up in the dark, like rocks suddenly come to life. As we approached, one of them began to lope toward the woods. The second groundhog paused and then chased after the first. I opened the truck door and Mulligan tore out across the yard after them. I watched him run, but the groundhogs made the edge of the trees before he was halfway there.

It looked like someone had dropped a grenade in the garden patch. Half-eaten onions lay scattered across the soil, and a short trench, where the carrots had been planted, stretched in shadows in the dirt. Roots from the leek plants were tangled around the makeshift wooden stands, snapped in two. We could hear Mulligan's barking from down the driveway, and the scent of the loose earth hovered above the wreckage, sweet and sharp.

Jake stood behind the truck as I poked at some of the carrots, bits and pieces missing, and their long, stringy roots wrapped in knots.

"That's a lot of hard work ruined," he said.

"Yeah."

He walked up the driveway after Mulligan and left me kneeling in the soil. I picked up a string of carrots, half-grown, and wiped at them. In the shed I switched the light on and found the trowel and the shovel, slinging them over my shoulder with the two empty buckets. I returned a few minutes later and dragged a heavy bag of fresh soil along the pathway. With the moon gone it was dark in the patch, but some of the brighter stars were beginning to appear on the horizon. Jake's boots crunched in the gravel down near the woods. I knelt in the soil and began to separate the vegetables, making two piles in the corners.

Fixing torn-up divots in the outfield at the baseball stadium was good practice for the job. I was already making calculations in my head—the number of bulbs I still had in the house, how much time I had before winter, which rows, as a whole, might be replanted, and where I might get some wire fencing to put up around the garden.

Jake walked up to the patch, and Mulligan trotted behind him, his head hung low, defeated. Jake stood with one hand in his pocket, the other holding an envelope face down. "Grady," he said.

I went back to separating the vegetables. "What's that?"

"It's for you."

I took the letter from him, smearing soil across the parchment. The return address was from Frank Wood Hospital, Arizona, but it was addressed to Jake, not me.

"It's for you," I said, handing it back.

"But it's about you."

"Take it."

He frowned but closed his fingers around it, pausing and then tearing the paper up the side. He slipped a letter out and unfolded it. Turning in place, he tried to catch some of the light from the stars, and I could see his eyes squinting and trying to focus. In the woods, two pigeons called back and forth to one another, seeming to send the same message. Jake stood for a few moments and then handed it to me.

"My eyes aren't good enough," he said.

I took the letter from him and read it, pausing word by

word, trying to make out sentences in the starlight. Mulligan sniffed at the onions in the garden, and Jake lit up a cigarette, the first spark of tobacco mixing with the scent of the soil.

After a time, I folded the letter up and stuck it in my pocket. I picked up the trowel and began scooping dirt back into the short trench.

"Go through that pile," I said, motioning to the rest of the vegetables. "Pick out anything that seems like it's worth saving."

I knelt in the dirt and dug new holes in the earth. Jake brought pails of water from inside the house and a stack of wood from behind the shed. He set the cords of wood one by one on a bigger log, splitting them in thirds down the side with a hatchet. With the hammer from the truck cab, he pounded the fresh stakes around the edge of the garden, making a wall a foot and a half high. On the corners were longer stakes, like the towers of a frontier fort. While I replanted the carrots and onions, dropping seeds into fresh holes, Jake disappeared inside and returned later with an armful of wire hangers. He clipped them near the top with wire cutters, twisted them together, and ran them like string from the four corners of the fence.

We worked all night, stopping only to share coffee from a thermos. When the orange glow from the sun appeared over the mountains, I had to squint from the brightness. All night long we'd worked in the light from stars.

I remembered then something my mom had told me: The first star at night appears like a point on a map—the only point—and from that position, other stars emerge. They scatter in unpredictable places, depending on where you are, and they create meaningful constellations. When the sky becomes full, at the latest hour of the night, it's easy to pick out the dominant star—Vega some nights, Polaris on others. But it's difficult to remember, looking up at the map, which star came first—which one was the point that held the rest in place.

You think to yourself: Which one of those stars up there shined the brightest, when it mattered the most?

George Stolz

*This photograph of me and my mother was taken
at the peak of Hawk Mountain, in eastern
Pennsylvania, in the mid-1960s. It was taken by
my maternal grandfather, whose long shadow falls
at the bottom of the frame. Elsewhere, also.*

George Stolz's work has been published in the *Atlantic Monthly*, the *Antioch
Review*, the *New York Times*, and other publications. This is his second story
published in *Glimmer Train*: "The Boy Who Lay Down" was published in the
Summer 1999 issue. He lives with his wife and two young sons in Madrid,
where he is currently putting the finishing touches on a short-story collection.

GEORGE STOLZ
The Man in the Moon

abriel Pierce, toddler son in tow, was drifting back through the empty cobblestoned streets of the city's old quarter at the midday *siesta* hour of meal and rest. The same neighborhood had been bustling only a short while before; when he had dropped his wife off at the Overseas American Women's Club pre-Easter Benefit Bazaar, there had been so many people spilling off the narrow sidewalks into the likewise narrow streets that the outnumbered cars were forced to nudge their way along, advancing only as the pedestrians permitted—no point in honking, no hope of hurrying the tarrying crowds. Unaccompanied old women on their way to Saturday market, some bloated and thick, others tough and leathery, all of them toting some sort of basket or cart. Flushed, well-fed boys with soccer balls gathered at the empty lots, their cries like the cries of gulls. An overflow crowd at a storefront bakery, harvesting big round loaves of fresh bread by the armload. Old men greeting each other by shouting into each other's faces. Navigating through the middle of it all, a team of street sweepers, uniformed and cheerful and utterly ineffectual.

And now? Now it was not so much that Pierce seemed to have stepped into a different city; he seemed to have shifted into a different era. With the streets shorn of life, the buildings looked aged and deteriorated in ways that usually went unnoticed, just as a face that falls suddenly still in disappointment or anger or simple inattentiveness will just as suddenly appear much, much older. How could so many doors and shutters be shut at once? How could an entire neighborhood agree to such unison silence? How could so much life, so many lives, agree to one single, shared rhythm? Was this perhaps just the sort of thing that makes up an authentic society, the sort of extended rules that make up extended families?

Silence. Family.

Yet despite their deep well of quiet, the streets were not muffled; to the contrary, their shuttered, flat-faced narrowness produced an amplified resonance that allowed the progress of hard-soled shoes striking cobblestones to be followed from a distance, that caused people to lower their voices instinctively. Even Pierce's little son sensed this and had lowered the volume of his streaming alliterative babble. The boy played with words the whole day through, turning them into quasi-physical things as he moved them around in his mouth, shaping them and then changing their shapes, arranging them in extended tropes based only on their intrinsic tone and overtone, their music and echo, all but freed from the shackled sequences of meaning: *beurre, beurre, bird, bird, butter, butter, beurre, beurre.*

Pierce glanced down at his son; his son, in response, flung both arms straight up in the air, elbows locked, tiny fingers splayed, head thrown back, a brusque, full-bodied movement like that of an orchestra conductor signalling the release of a finale. The proportions of his small body were those of toddlerhood; his upraised hands barely reached beyond the top of his puppy-like, too-large head. The gesture meant that he wanted to be picked up and carried—he was tired after so much toddling. Pierce hitched the boy sidesaddle onto his hip. The tiny knees gripped his side, a warm moist hand rested on the back of Pierce's neck. Being parent to a small child brought with it an unanticipated increase in informal physical contact, in direct skin-to-skin communication. Pierce and his wife got along well enough, but they didn't crawl all over one another whenever they had the chance. They didn't pull on each other's noses or probe each other's gums with dirty fingers. They didn't sit in each other's laps in order to page through picture books and magazines. They rarely fell asleep on each other's shoulders.

With the toddler in his arms, Pierce's pace quickened; soon he found himself following unfamiliar narrow streets around unfamiliar corners. As if in response to the question forming itself in his mind, he heard a church bell toll the half-hour; there was still time to kill before joining his wife. He had finished most of his own Saturday day-off errands sooner than planned. He fingered the unmailed envelope in his jacket pocket: the post office, along with most everything else in this old-fashioned part of the city, had already closed. Nothing to do but wait. He had been stationed in Europe for more than three years, and this business of shuttling his wife around on weekends and then dealing with the ensuing state of enforced idleness until she had finished her visits was still one of the greatest novelties of the life they had chosen. This sort of thing didn't happen when there were two cars in a family. It didn't happen when both halves of a couple worked. It didn't happen when lives weaved in and out according to intricately coordinated schedules, parallel and independent, coinciding only as planned beforehand in staggered, rationed shifts. In other words, it didn't happen in America.

Which of course was the whole idea to begin with. Which of course was what his wife had wanted, why she had given up her own career and had coaxed Pierce to accept an overseas transfer; otherwise she was afraid she would probably never get pregnant. She was probably right.

When the bell tolled the half-hour for the second time Pierce succeeded in locating it in its belfry; his eye automatically scanned the rest of the building until it reached the church's entrance. The entrance was modest—no grand stone steps, no arches or carved figures. Just a street-level post-and-lintel door, thick and almost rustic, blackened with soot and exhaust fumes and age, most likely oak of the sort that no longer grew anymore, anywhere. The door was curiously simple, yet even more curious than the door itself was the fact

that it was open; even churches were usually closed for business at this hour, sealed imposingly tight, sometimes even
brandishing heavy chains and padlocks—always a jarring image. Still carrying the boy, Pierce pushed the door open a bit
further and entered; his wife never failed to observe on such
occasions that in Europe they spent more time than ever
going into churches without ever actually going to church.
Once inside, three black stone steps descended into the central nave. Pierce saw that he had entered through a side door,
not through the main entrance, which explained the door's
simplicity. He also saw why the church was open and its lights
lit; there was a baptism taking place.

The baptizing family was clustered around the altar at the
front of the church; there were too few family members to
occupy the vast pews or to counteract the church's dwarfing
scale. A young, washed-out-looking priest, robed in green
and white, was conducting the baptism. The mother held the
bundled baby high in her arms, trying to keep the swaddling
blankets in place, trying to keep the tired, heavily made-up
smile fixed on her face. A disproportionate number of the
other family members were young men, an abundance of
uncles, boisterous boy-men on their best behavior, beefy as
bodyguards and unsure of where to put their hands. One of
the uncles, the youngest of them, handled the video camera,
never removing it from in front of his face, never turning off
the machine. There were few older people in attendance and
no other small children whatsoever; the newborn baby was
the first of a new and presumably diminishing generation.

None of them seemed to notice Pierce's entrance: the
mother kept her eyes on the precarious blankets; the younger
brother continued ducking and gliding, zooming and reced-
ing; the wan young priest continued reciting as the others
continued listening conscientiously. Pierce turned in the opposite direction and started making his away around the rest

of the church, surveying the framed paintings and frescoed ceilings in the side chapels. But his attention was still drawn toward the baptism. He paused at the back of the church and looked again toward the group gathered at the altar. What would happen if Pierce were to rush up the main aisle to the front of the church and demand that his as-yet-unbaptized son be baptized too? The family would be horrified, and understandably so. Pierce suspected that those thick boy-men might shed their best manners and suit jackets in a hurry and forcibly remove him and his son from the church, unconcerned whether he were devotion-struck or mad or just an uncouth foreigner. They might even turn off the video camera—wonder of wonders. But wouldn't the washed-out-looking young priest have to accede, horrified or not? Wouldn't he be obliged by history and church law and hard demographic reality to save a little one's soul, or any soul at all for that matter, regardless of its provenance?

The maneuver, although rash, would at least provide an instant resolution to a problem that Pierce and his wife seemed incapable of resolving any other way. Despite their own entrenched religious apathy, they both favored baptizing their son—it would be easier for him, when the inevitable time came, to discard than to acquire. Yet they never succeeded in arranging the event itself. Each time they attempted to do so, each time they addressed the logistics in earnest, they were tripped up by the question of godparents. It was a simple, one-syllable question: who? Neither Pierce nor his wife had established outside relationships that were sufficiently intimate, not from among Pierce's co-workers nor from among the chattering older couples at his wife's club. Yet simply choosing the nearest at hand seemed unacceptable and even somehow wrong, particularly given the already tenuous foundations of faith underpinning the oft-proposed, oft-postponed event.

No one was born a Christian: that was the real problem. Christianity was not an ethnicity. It was not a nationality. It was not a clan. Every Christian had to convert or be converted: that was baptism itself, a watery conversion. Yet even the children of illegal immigrants were not themselves illegal—born in America, American. Born in France, French. Even blind parents engender seeing children.

Pierce turned away from the altar and resumed his absent-minded study of the side chapels, stroking his son's hair and enjoying the stillness that always seemed to bathe the boy in the hush of holy places. Pierce and his wife had initially planned on baptizing him as an infant during their last visit back home, in Pierce's parents' church, with Pierce's younger brother as the sole godparent. But that plan had come to bust. They hadn't booked the church well enough in advance, their visit became hectic and overloaded with more pressing and complicated concerns, and finally Pierce and his brother had had a terrible falling out, so severe that they had parted without speaking to each other.

They still weren't talking; the stamped, addressed, and still-unmailed envelope in Pierce's pocket was proof that the rift had not yet healed, even now, even after Pierce's mother had telephoned them in order to let them know about his brother's condition. Pierce's wife, who barely knew his brother, had cried; Pierce hadn't. And his wife was the one who had prepared a set of baby pictures to send—an open gesture of reconciliation. Pierce had even gotten as far as the post office with the addressed envelope of pictures, where he was going to enclose a short note. But standing at the inclined writing surface in the post office, trying to compose the note, trying just to let a few meaningless, handwritten words of greeting spill out onto the unlined sheet of notepaper, he had found himself unable.

What would he say? What could he possibly say? "I'm sorry

you have AIDS"? He would have to do better than that. Perhaps just "I'm sorry." But sorry for what? Not for anything he, Pierce, had done.

Perhaps for what he had left undone?

No, not that either.

Just sorry. Sorry for us all. Sorry for the fundamental sorriness of this sorry life, for all the sorry-ass creatures in this sorry tomb of a world.

And even that would not have been enough.

Better to say nothing at all, as usual. But to send the pictures alone was unthinkable. Pierce knew how unsettling it would be to tear open an envelope and find oneself dealt a poker hand's worth of beautiful family photos, pictures of a beautiful child in beautiful light looking straight at the camera with a beautifully limpid gaze, yet to receive them as if tossed, unaccompanied by any message, unassuaged by any willed sign of life from the sender. The absence would jolt, would give a different message, unintended and liable to be misconstrued.

Pierce became aware of the incipient ache in his arm; he set his son back down on the floor and continued meandering among the church's many side chapels. The boy stayed close by Pierce's side, holding loosely onto Pierce's pinky. Pierce's brother used to do the same when they were little and in unfamiliar places, on a trip or attending some intimidating formal affair with their parents, or sometimes just walking down the street together. The image was sweet to envision from the perspective of memory: a small boy and a smaller boy, the explicit acceptance of biggerness and littlerness, the child-scale give and take of guidance and protection. It was sweet, but Pierce's memories of that sort were few. There had been too many years between him and his brother, too many years and no other siblings to generate a fuller emotional geometry within the large clean rooms of their childhood. What he remembered with greater vividness was a constant linear sense of distrust. Even while they sat in the same room playing with the same toys, or as they were both doing their homework, or as they lay in their beds reading—it was always there. Distrust, and, as a consequence, vigilance. As if he and his brother were watching each other. Watching carefully. Watching across a distance. Watching as if in judgment.

After what his brother had done, after Pierce had read what his brother had written—was it possible that his imagination was working retroactively, ascribing their later estrangement to those defenseless childhood memories? No, those feelings had been there, and had been mutual. That book—his brother's book—was proof, if nothing else. Pierce had read it in its entirety in one single, dumbstruck sitting on his last trip home, nauseated by the essays and memoirs his brother had published about their shared childhood and youth, about Pierce himself, and especially about their parents. Dumbstruck and hurt. It was one thing for his brother to make the world a witness to his struggle toward a sexual identity, and to make that sexual identity a part of the public domain. That was all fine and good. But for some reason his brother must have felt that the telling of it lacked an element of drama, and in order to provide it, he needed a caricatured backdrop; so he portrayed the rest of the family as the villains they were not and never had been, as mere foils, ridiculous and hysterical, sometimes even cartoonish. It was a cheap trick, a television or vaudeville device.

But it was also their life.

It was impossible for Pierce to believe that his brother really saw them that way, them or the life they had spent together. That hadn't been necessary. Their life had not been like that—life was not like that. And then, on top of it all, for all that oh-so-fine, oh-so-eloquently rendered writing, his brother had not written or even called to tell him what had happened or what was happening. Or what would happen.

Pierce realized that his son was signalling to him, tugging at his finger and calling "Papa? Papa?" in a light voice, the lightest of voices, the sort of insistent whisper of which only a child is capable. When the boy was certain of Pierce's attention he pointed up toward the fresco painted into the ceiling of the chapel they had entered, a busy baroque constellation of angels hovering in a chipped indigo night sky. "Button?" the boy asked in the same soft voice, pronouncing it as "bu-un?," a Hottentot stop separating the syllables into two discontinuous sounds. "Button?" Pierce saw that the boy was pointing to the painted moon, simple and white and round amid the angels—Well, yes, why not? The moon as a button, the button of the night, buttoned up snug in its button hole, keeping the big bad night shut tight. Why not? He could believe almost anything about the moon. Years before, during the summer of the first lunar landing, Pierce and his brother lay together in the meadow behind the vacation cabin that their parents rented each year and stared hard at the moon; they were looking for the men on the moon. Eventually, through the all-potent combination of desire and suggestion and television, they began to see the American astronauts landing on the moon. They lay side by side in the July grass, big brother and little brother, secure in their knowledge that no one else could hear them, and described out loud what they and only they saw happening way up there on the moon's surface. Spaceships spewing rings of orange-and-blue flame. Arcing signal flares. Bulky white-suited figures tramping across the dusty lunar craters. And look, there, an American flag—it's not drooping, of course it's not, there's tons of wind out there, silly.

The men on the moon.

I see them! I see them! Do you see them? Do you?

Yes.

Pierce's little brother went on to become an astronomy

buff, reading and studying constellation maps and staring for hours at the night sky, connecting the dots into figures and patterns that no one else in their family was ever able to follow. Pierce's chosen hobby at that time was trees; he could recite the identifying characteristics and Latin names of every single one of the trees that ringed the meadow. One afternoon toward the end of that same summer, the summer of '69, Pierce sat in the center of the meadow with his grandmother. His grandmother was by that time weepy and slightly incoherent, smelling of balms and medicines and other unpleasant things. She had held onto both of Pierce's hands and stared dimly off at the trees around the meadow, and cried as she went on and on about what trees had been like when she was a girl, and about the ravages of the blights that had struck in the years that followed. Pierce eventually began crying with her, crying without quite knowing why he was crying, crying even though he was trying his hardest not to, while his grandmother, engrossed in her own memories and visions, didn't even seem to notice his tears. He hadn't enjoyed the session with his grandmother much, but when school resumed in September, he voluntarily wrote a research report on the tree epidemics of the early century, the chestnut blight and Dutch elm disease. He pored over the encyclopedias in the school library, recounting the futile federal eradication programs of the thirties and forties, tracing illustrations onto sheets of onion-skin paper, and furnishing a detailed description of how the blights functioned. They attacked the younger, most vigorous trees first, poisoning their veins, preying on them not when they were saplings, but rather waiting until they had passed through the most vulnerable period, until the moment when they were at their most ascendent, strangling them from within at their point of fullest promise. Still the most graceful, they were never to reach their full height and might, their full glory, never to fulfill that promise. Instead, they were the first to die.

I'm sorry.

The baby at the altar emitted a short shrill cry of discomfort that soared through the church's upper reaches. A wave of tittering laughter and shifting limbs followed. The baptism was coming to a close. Pierce scooped his son up again and left the chapel, heading back across the church toward the side door through which they had first come. Halfway there he paused and looked over the baptismal scene one last time; the anonymous, insentient little bundle at the center of it all could just as easily have contained a doll or a dog or cat as a baby. The young priest made a slow, stylized sign of the cross over it. Behind him the church's tremendous altarpiece, gleaming with gilt, rose up nearly to the ceiling, its profusion of obsessive baroque ornamentation covering every last bit of available surface area. *Horror vacuii*: fear of emptiness, horror in the face of the void. The void—like the night? No, not like the night; not like the unadorned night, not like the moon and stars adrift across the big empty night. Pierce felt his own chest emptying too quickly, emptying of breath, swelling and falling dangerously. As if trying to prop himself up, to brace his failing shoulders and vertebrae, he crossed himself. Why not? If he could believe in the man in the moon, he could believe almost anything. He moved his free hand as slowly as the young priest had over the baby, trying by force of will to internalize the rectilinear structure he was tracing, to install it, even temporarily, within himself; before he had completed the gesture he saw that his son was already attempting to imitate him. Feigning a fierce look of concentration that Pierce suddenly saw must be a deformed reflection of his own grimacing countenance, the boy bunched his fingers together into an awkward sort of fist and then moved it with surprising precision—back and forth, up and down—across his shoulders and chest; he repeated the gesture, again and again, each time with greater fluidity but with diminishing accuracy until eventually he was swinging his hand around in a lopsided circle. When he sensed that he was being watched he stopped and looked up; making eye contact with Pierce, he burst out laughing.

VIKRAM CHANDRA
Writer

Interview
by Jennifer Levasseur
and Kevin Rabalais

Vikram Chandra was born in New Delhi, India, in 1961. He briefly attended St. Xavier's College in Bombay before moving to the United States to study creative writing at Pomona College in Claremont, California. After graduating in 1984, he attended Columbia University's film school. He left before completing his degree to begin the novel Red Earth and Pouring Rain. *He worked on the*

Vikram Chandra

novel while a student of John Barth at Johns Hopkins and, later, of Donald Barthelme at the University of Houston. Red Earth and Pouring Rain *was awarded the David Higham Prize for Fiction and the Commonwealth Writers Prize for Best First Published Book.* Love and Longing in Bombay, *a collection of*

Glimmer Train Stories, Issue 40, Fall 2001
© *2001 Jennifer Levasseur and Kevin Rabalais*

stories, followed. It won the Commonwealth Prize for Best Book (Eurasia region), was included in the **New York Times Book Review**'s *"Notable Books of 1997" and was short-listed for the Guardian Fiction Prize. The story "Dharma," included in the collection, won the* **Paris Review**'s *Discovery Prize. In 1997, the* **New Yorker** *listed Chandra as one of "India's leading novelists." He divides his time between Bombay and Washington, D.C., where he is a professor of creative writing at George Washington University.*

In Red Earth and Pouring Rain, *you use your Indian heritage and American experience to create two distinct styles of writing. The Indian sections employ epic, lyrical storytelling, while the American ones explore pop culture and student life. How did you balance these almost opposing styles while writing the novel?*

It became clear as I started the book that all sorts of epic Indian story-within-story forms were going to be present. And I also wanted to deploy the forms more familiar to the modern, Western reader, the sort of narrative found in the *New Yorker*, all smooth surfaces with a beginning, middle, tiny epiphany and end. I wanted these forms to interrogate each other, to create a kind of juxtapositional irony. This also allowed me to juxtapose a longer sentence, such as the ones in the Indian parts, which curve in and out, and a short, clipped sentence, like those in the American sections. Part of the thematic and aesthetic intent was to create this electric charge between different narrative modes, and it was fun to do. I didn't want to allow any of the forms or kinds of language to have an unquestioned authority, an unchallenged claim to the truth. The two modes, by being in the same space at the same time, question each other.

Do you think of these styles as two sides of yourself as a writer?

Well, Indian traditions and the West, or the West in India, are very much agents within the life of modern Indians. Both narratives are present in post-independence India, and modern India is a hybrid created at the intersection of these narratives. This juxtaposition, this hybridity, presents itself in several ways, all the time. You see old cities in India that to Western eyes don't look like cities at all. And you have the newer parts of the cities that date back to British times, which are built at right angles and are planned in a Western sense. There are certain types of narratives held within those two kinds of landscapes. I think that when the British started building in India, the old city was incomprehensible to them in all its layerings. The new cities— this can be seen in Delhi and Calcutta—were supposed to embody a different way of perceiving time and history and the ways people are supposed to relate to each other. When you grow up in Delhi, you move through these various cities, through these different ways of being.

Did you write the Indian sections first and then move on to the American ones?

No, the book was written as it was published, which is to say that I wrote one Indian chapter, then one American chapter, and so on. This was actually quite pleasurable, the movement from the long sentences of the Indian sections to the short sentences of the American bits and back. Just as I'd start to get bored with one, it would be time to move to the other. I did move some sections around after I'd finished the first draft.

You moved to the United States to attend school. As a film student at Columbia University, you stumbled upon the autobiography of Colonel James "Sikander" Skinner, who was a half-Indian and half-British 19th century soldier. You used his book as the basis for Red Earth and Pouring Rain. *How did you know this idea was a novel and not a film?*

One of the interesting things about that autobiography is that Skinner originally dictated it in Persian. A friend of his translated it into English. As you read it, the friend's narration jumps into the middle of Skinner's text from time to time and says, "Okay, I'm going to move you ahead two years." And you say, "Wait, I want to know what happened in those two years." You can see the translator's reshaping hand, which obviously has an explicit political, ideological intent. The man's life is reshaped through the translation into something that stands as a monument to the British imperial cause. So you sense that Skinner's voice is not quite getting through to you; you are only hearing a version of it. And also, you must remember that at the time, Persian was the language of state affairs, of legal matters. On the street, every day, Skinner would've spoken Hindustani, a hybrid tongue. By telling his story in Persian, he is already translating. All these questions of language are brought home to you the moment you start to read that book. So, language, translation, modes of narrative—all of these are essential parts of the very fabric of *Red Earth and Pouring Rain*. I knew instantly that this wasn't something I could do in film. It was something that had to be written, that could exist only as a book.

What aspects from your background in film have you used in your writing?

When I write, the image comes first. By image, I mean something that is quite cinematic, so I might see a scene, the people in it, and how they move in relation to one another— what they say, what they do to each other. The struggle becomes how to translate the feeling of that movement onto the page so that the reader lives the story that was in my head. I don't know if other writers do it differently, but that seems to be how stories come to me.

I'm certain, also, that I've absorbed lessons about texture, pacing and scale from Indian films. Indian commercial films are all musicals. You can have a very violent film in which people are shooting each other, but at some point they stop and somebody sings a song. My brother-in-law, Vinod Chopra, is a filmmaker, and he made a film several years ago called *Parinda* ("Bird") about gangsters in Bombay. It's gritty, but occasionally the action stops, the narrative shifts into a lyrical mode, and somebody sings. To an eye trained by Western musical comedies or romances, this doesn't make any sense. But in India, war movies can be musicals. A recent film about the 1971 war with Pakistan was called *Border*. Some of the sequences in this film are quite brutal, but these characters, these soldiers awaiting combat at the edge of the desert, sing songs. That movement between different modes, from the very gritty to the lyrical, is something that I grew up with. The origins of this structure are very old, and one finds analogous narrative movements in ancient Indian epics, in classical Sanskrit drama, in popular Indian theater. Classical Indian texts on aesthetics advise the poet to wisely mingle various emotional states, to use music and dance to heighten the viewer's pleasure, his or her immersion into the internal life of the characters. So this is something that's quite traditional, and it finds its most obvious contemporary expression in films, which I happen to have seen a lot of. My family is a filmmaking family: my mother is a screenwriter; one sister, Tanuja, is a screenwriter and director; another sister, Anupama, is a film critic married to a film producer and director.

What was your family's reaction when you decided to leave India and study filmmaking and writing?

They were always encouraging, especially my father. My mother was somewhat more skeptical, having herself been a writer. She knew exactly how hard it would be to make a living from writing. My earliest memories are of her sitting at the kitchen table, writing. She wrote and acted for Indian television during its infancy in Delhi in the '60s. She also wrote for radio and, later, for film in the '70s. She understood my urgent desire to write, but was afraid of how hard it would be. In India, during the '60s and '70s, it made no sense to think you were going to be a writer. In the '80s, after the success enjoyed by Salman Rushdie and others, everyone began to see it as a possibility, as a viable job or vocation that people could have. Before that, if you said you were going to be a writer, the immediate response was, "That's nice. What else are you going to do?"

Who are some of the writers you read growing up?

The first stories I remember hearing are tales from the great Indian epics, the *Mahabharat* and the *Ramayana*, which my mother, my grandmothers and my aunts told to me. I grew these stories into my bones, and I live with them still. Once I started to go to school, I read an eclectic mixture of Indian and Western authors. I read R. K. Narayan, Khuswant Singh and Raja Rao, and later, Salman Rushdie, Anita Desai and Amitav Ghosh. I remember reading an abridged version of *The Adventures of Huckleberry Finn* in fifth grade, and went on from there to read Wharton, Fitzgerald and Hemingway. In college, I started reading British novelists, and I am still a passionate admirer of Trollope and Thackeray.

In "Dharma," from Love and Longing in Bombay, *your character Subramaniam, who narrates all the stories in the collection, says, "Some people need their ghosts, and some don't, but we are all haunted by them." He is energized by the stories he hears. In your stories and novel, you remind us that everyone has a story. You seem to want to tell these stories and show these characters, no matter how minor they seem at first.*

Even the most ordinary lives, once you begin to press on them a little, reveal themselves to be full of the most affecting pathos. It is certainly tempting, as a storyteller, to play with the larger-than-life characters and landscapes of *Red Earth and Pouring Rain*. But it is also satisfying to tell the kinds of stories that Subramaniam does in *Love and Longing in Bombay*. He seems to listen to the stories that some very ordinary people tell, the kinds of men and women who your glance might pass over easily in a local train in Bombay. And he discovers that the ordinary isn't very ordinary, after all. My temptation as a writer is to investigate all these stories, to tie them together in the mesh they make in the world.

Some critics have labeled Love and Longing in Bombay *a novel. There is a similar structure to the stories, and they are all linked by the same narrator. Did you visualize this book as a collection of stories or a novel?*

The stories in *Love and Longing in Bombay* are self-contained, even though they are told by the same narrator. They exist in the same physical landscape, and resonate with each other, but they don't depend on each other in terms of narrative logic. In *Red Earth and Pouring Rain*, all the various narratives flow together and depend on each other. So it's more of a novel than *Love and Longing in Bombay*, although I must say that I'm not tremendously invested in hewing to one idea of what a "novel" should be. Or, for that matter, what a "short story" should be. I tell stories. Maybe the forms some of these stories find don't fit neatly into any category.

In Red Earth and Pouring Rain, *the characters use stories to say things they would not otherwise disclose. What do you think stories enable us to do?*

Stories let us say things that we might otherwise censor, hide even from ourselves. So, we tell secrets in stories, but we also say that which is unsayable. Life visits upon us the tragedy of passing days, the inescapable death that comes to us, the unfairness of history and suffering—and in stories we shape this chaos; we form our relationship with all these inexplicable, unsayable things. We do not vanquish the chaos, this *asat*, but we speak to it with *sat*, truth.

Red Earth and Pouring Rain *was written on an epic scale, using hundreds of characters and weaving stories throughout. How did you keep everything in focus?*

I've tended, in the past, not to do much outlining, which is strange, considering the kind of books I've produced. I have tried doing it, but it doesn't work very well for me. I find outlines confining, and in any case it becomes hard to represent the resonance of image, language and theme that I'm most interested in. *Red Earth and Pouring Rain* was written over six years, and somehow over that long time I was able to keep the geometry of the book clear in my head. There was, of course, the historical record to point me in certain directions; the major events of Sikander Skinner's life provided a natural structure that I was able to follow. In general, however, I start with an image, a resonant visual image that stays with me. And I have some sense of the feeling of the end of the story, where I want to end up. Then I discover what lies between this beginning and end.

What was your editing process for the novel?

After I finished the first draft, I left it completely alone for five months. I'd lived with it for such a long time that it had become something of a joke with my friends in Houston and Bombay, Vikram's endless novel. I needed to be able to detach myself from it for a bit. Then I came back and read it again. My friend Alexis Quinlan read it at the same time, and she had some suggestions. Then I went back through the entire manuscript and did a pretty close edit. After Penguin/India accepted the book, my editor there, David Davidar, had some important ideas about the structure of the book, which I found useful. I spent a couple months moving things around, looking for resonance and clarity, and then finally the manuscript seemed quite stable.

Are you able to write whenever you sit down?

No. There are mornings when I don't have anything, when I've reached a certain point in the narrative and I don't know what is going to happen next. I sit there and wait for it to form itself. It's not something I can quite shape; it has to come to me. Sometimes, a month will go by when nothing happens. This is scary, but there is nothing I can do about it.

In Red Earth and Pouring Rain, *Sanjay says to Abhay, "The stories cease to be yours the moment you write them down." What is your relationship with your characters after you have completed a book?*

It's like sending children out into the world, really. It's difficult to control how other people see them or react to them or engage with them. I did mean that when I wrote it, that stories cease to be yours the moment you write them down, and I still agree with Sanjay. What the characters become when they are out in the world is sometimes strange and foreign from what I intended them to be. They get rewritten, reinscribed, in the lives of my readers. I still feel close to those characters, but they change, and I change. I was looking at *Red Earth and Pouring Rain* the other day and thinking that it feels like it was written by somebody else. You get distant from the person who started the book.

How do you respond to criticism of your work?

I hear of writers who say that they never read their reviews, but I find myself interested in them. They are, after all, reactions to my work, albeit from a group of readers who are hugely overworked, overfed with books to a point well beyond satiation, and who are obliged to have an opinion about fifteen times a week. So, I read the critics, but with a very large dose of salt. You can't get too happy about a good review or be destroyed by a bad one. It's important to remember that early reviews are generally wrong about great works of art, or even about good ones. These early reactions might make some sort of immediate difference in sales, but the life of a book is much longer than the life of a critic, and your work will find its own way in the world. I think you have to be skeptical about reviews in general, and keep yourself close to the ground and keep on working. Remember the pleasure of the work, and keep on working.

A few years ago, the New Yorker *published an issue dedicated to*

Indian writing. In an article in that issue, Salman Rushdie wrote, "[India feels] like a non-stop assault on the senses, the emotions, the imagination, and the spirit." Was there a conscious attempt in Love and Longing in Bombay *to present the sensual elements of India for the reader?*

I think I agree with Salman, although that assault is also, simultaneously, an overflow of energy. In this churning, there is also sustenance and growth. Bombay is a ferocious city, a monster that eats its children alive. And yet, there is a dynamism that flows in its streets, a jostling energy and large-heartedness that is good to be near. I hope that in *Love and Longing in Bombay* my love for the city is apparent.

In that issue of the New Yorker, *there is a photograph of you with Vikram Seth, Salman Rushdie, Anita Desai, Amitav Ghosh and Arundhati Roy, among others. What do you think about being grouped with those considered to be India's leading novelists?*

It was odd that most of us hadn't met each other before that morning the photograph was taken. It's a reflection, of course, of the tremendous diaspora of Indians across the globe. A lot of voices are speaking from scattered places. It was good to come together in London for that photograph, to meet one's fellow travelers.

With the recent fiftieth anniversary of Indian independence, what do you think about the strong surge of fiction written in English coming from young Indian writers?

I grew up in an India where I spoke English on the playground, in school, and at home, with an abiding sense that this was a language that belonged to me. There was a colonial past, but in the most immediate sense, I wrote in English because it was the language that came naturally off my tongue. The work that is being written in English in India represents one kind of Indian voice finding its range and strength. There is some good work being done. I should say, also, that there are many, many wonderful writers in the other Indian languages. They are being increasingly translated into English, but not enough.

What is your relationship with India now?

I spend five, maybe five and a half, months in India every year. Bombay and India are home to me. I think of myself as an expatriate Indian writer, although the United States is like a second home for me. I've spent many of my growing-up years here, and I'm deeply connected to it. I intend to keep going back and forth. I think, also, that going away from India remains useful for me. The disengagement allows all of those elements I absorb from Indian landscapes to settle, so I can start to see them imaginatively and shape them. The distance helps. I suppose writers, artists of every sort, from all over the world, have done this. You go away from where your material is to get some distance on it. The book I'm working on now stays within India, but I'm sure I will write about America and the West again.

What are the differences between writing when you're living in America and when you're living in India?

I get about the same amount of writing done in Bombay and America. But Bombay, for me, is a much more distracting city; there's always something going on, and there's always some new layer of it that I have to discover. It seduces me constantly. In D.C., I lead a much quieter life: I teach at the university; I go home. I'm by no means a hermit. I do go out, but I don't have that sort of passionate love for this landscape as I do for Bombay. So I'm able to resist it more. I suspect I've structured my life this way, to find a balance. But in both places, I find the time to work.

You wrote parts of Red Earth and Pouring Rain *under the direction of John Barth and Donald Barthelme. What did you learn from these writers?*

It was wonderful. Jack Barth and I shared a sort of sympathy in that he was a writer of a certain kind of metafiction that was also substantial and epic in its concern. I had read his books before going to study with him. I liked the magnificent intelligence in his books and the playfulness with form. Working with him was encouraging, revivifying. I think he understood what I was trying to get at, and he was very generous with his time and also in his praise of the potential of what I was trying to do. I had just started *Red Earth and Pouring Rain*. I mean that literally; I'd thought about the book for quite a while, but I wrote the first page on the first day of the semester. I brought in the first hundred pages or so into his classes as the workshop progressed. He encouraged me to keep writing. At that point, when I was struggling to find my voice—and I was not sure if what I was doing was any good at all—even the smallest word had the power to keep me going for years and years. It was very good of him to do that.

The Johns Hopkins writing program was only one year long, so Jack asked me what I was going to do afterward. At that point, I hadn't even managed to get my protagonist, Sikander Skinner, born, so it was obvious the story was going to be longer than I'd thought it was. So Jack said, "Maybe you should think of going to Houston." Donald Barthelme taught there, at the University of Houston, and he and Jack were friends.

The interaction with Don was different. His fiction was very different from what I was doing, in its extreme economy, in those sentences of his that turn on a dime. It was very different from the big, rousing melodrama I was trying to get at in *Red Earth and Pouring Rain*. We actually struggled with each other for quite a long time. I admired his work, and it was fun to be in his workshop and to learn the way he approached a text, the microscopic attention he paid to the rhythm of a sentence. To learn how to do that was good, but I thought, "This guy doesn't quite get what I'm reaching for." Which was fine, and I went along with the workshops. It was interesting being in those workshops because the students, my peers, didn't seem to have a handle on my work, either. There were a couple who were encouraging; the rest were sort of baffled. I thought, "Okay, this is how it's going to be." Toward the end of the last semester we worked together, I'd brought in a chapter from the novel. Donald walked into the workshop and clapped, applauded. That was quite stunning. Finally, I think he saw the shape of the novel.

He was generous in his applause and really astonishingly generous in practical ways. He introduced me to the person who is now my agent. He had money from the university for his own use, but he used it to buy a copy machine for the department. If you are living on a graduate student salary and you've got to make sixteen copies of a forty-page story, that can cost you some real money. He took care of stuff like that. There was also an emergency loan fund in the department, so if you were really in trouble at the end of the month, you could go in and ask for some money and the department would give it to you, no questions asked. He understood the struggles people went through to be there and tried to help the best he could. I shouldn't make him sound like a cuddly father figure—he was paternal, but in a fearsome way. He was intimidating, a big, tall man with piercing eyes. When you walked in and sat down in that workshop, you could feel the tension. He could be very fierce, although he had mellowed by the time I got there. But there were still all kinds of "fierce Don" stories. I did hear him tell somebody to burn his novel. The person had been bringing in endless chapters of a novel that just wasn't working, and finally, Don said to him: "Burn it."

Now that you are a professor of creative writing, how has your writing been affected?

It is a great privilege to make a living by talking about the kind of work I'm interested in, to be paid for engaging in a conversation about writing. Some of the students are good writers and serious about writing, and they teach me things

172

all the time. And they also keep me on my toes, keep me from becoming complacent about my judgements, my tastes and my politics. Being in a classroom has been very good for my work.

What do you believe is your role as a teacher?

I want to create a space in which a serious, close reading of each student's work can happen. Often, the best reader in class for a given student's work is not the teacher, but another student. So my job is to provide a certain amount of direction, to encourage them to work hard on each manuscript that comes into class, to help them listen to reactions to their work with detachment, humor and openness. The danger in workshops is that the young writer starts writing for the committee, to please the crowd, to gain the teacher's admiration. This is generally a danger for young artists; even if you've never stepped into a workshop, you can be frightened by the establishment, seduced by its rewards. So you must learn to protect your voice, to defend what is essential to you. My job as a teacher is to be honest, to help each student find his or her voice, as best I can.

Does using aspects of India and America in your fiction help in showing students the advantage of not only using what they know but also expanding into other areas?

There is that old truism that is much bandied about in writing classes, "Write what you know." But I think it's equally important to write what you don't know, to use your writing as an investigative tool, to essay out in your stories. I do very consciously try to expose the students to different modes of storytelling, to forms that they might not ordinarily encounter.

What are you writing now?

I'm working on a novel now. After finishing *Red Earth and Pouring Rain*, I consciously turned to a shorter form, partly out of relief of having finished a long project, and partly out of wanting to work on something I could finish every few months instead of every few years. I also felt I wanted to stretch a different set of muscles. Always, for me, it's much harder to write shorter than to write longer. Poetry would be hard for me to write. So once I'd tested myself against the discipline of the short story, I was ready for another long haul. But there is a connection in this new novel to the short stories: the protagonist in the new book is Sartaj Singh, the police inspector from *Love and Longing in Bombay.*

Would you talk about that project?

The book starts in Bombay, and then moves outward. The second chapter was published as "Eternal Don" in the *New Yorker* in the summer of 1997. In that section, Sartaj is trying to talk a famous Mafia Don out of his bunker-like hideout. The book is about the underworld in Bombay and the connections of the underworld to everything else. The book started as a sort of Mafia thriller, but has become much larger, in terms of its size and thematic concerns. So, I'm writing.

Your fiction places a strong emphasis on oral storytelling. Do you think you will continue to use this narrative style in your work?

This must be because the first stories I experienced were told to me, and because this experience was profoundly moving, so rich, and so heartbreaking and sustaining. All the old Indian epics use this structure of concentric storytellers, of having characters say, "I must tell you a story," and then slipping you down another level of narrative. This form is unimaginably rich to me, full of opportunity and pleasure and complexity and irony, and it *feels* familiar and venerable and a part of me. When I started to write *Red Earth and Pouring Rain*, this form came easily and naturally to me. In the book I'm working on now, I've moved away from this kind of structure, but there is still some of this delight in telling a story, in having a story move from one person to the other. This is an old pleasure, and an eternal one.

The Last Pages

*Howland sisters, dancing on a picnic table,
through venetian blinds, circa 1938.*

TOM KEALEY

Well, I feel like Tommy Beaver has said more about "Groundskeeping" in his illustration than I ever could with a few words. I guess I'd like to start by thanking him for capturing the tone and spark of the story in the faces of Jake, Grady, and Mulligan. Thanks, bud.

"What's in the letter that Grady gets?" That's the question that people seem to have about this story. To be honest with you, I really don't know. I can tell you this: I want anyone (you) who reads a story of mine to feel like a participant in that story. You took the time to read it, and I think that gives you a right to answer the questions for yourself. I want readers to feel engaged by my stories. I think people appreciate things they have to work for, more than things that are given to them without asking. I hope you enjoyed hanging out with Jake and Grady for a while. I enjoyed writing about them.

Tom Kealey

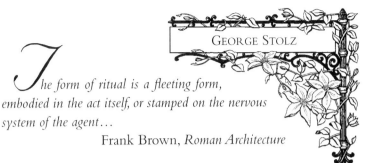

*The form of ritual is a fleeting form,
embodied in the act itself, or stamped on the nervous
system of the agent...*

Frank Brown, *Roman Architecture*

*The finest moment of the service, the best thing about
the altars and the empty aisles, was the moment when
you once more emerged into the sunlight and the door
closed behind you, and you were free, alive. That was the
only communicable experience.*

Cesare Pavese, *The House on the Hill*

*They're imitating the flamingos, which can be vaguely
made out in the background. Or, more likely, Jorge is
imitating the flamingos and Cristobal is imitating Jorge.*

MERRILL FEITELL

A couple of years ago I was driving through Texas when I had the very odd and awful experience of almost passing out at the wheel. Going to the hospital meant calling an ambulance to the middle of nowhere, abandoning a rental car, and missing a flight, all of which proved to be lonely, scary, and expensive, but it was obvious that there was no other choice—until I got home.

I somehow ended up far less worried about my physicality than about how I'd handled the whole thing. What if I'd just taken a nap on the side of the road or finished the trip with the windows rolled down? What if I'd never taken the trip at all? I started collecting opinions: What would you have done? What about you?

"Our Little Lone Star" grew less out of the whole weird medical incident than from the simple fact of all that grueling self-doubt.

It seems unjust to tell the story of this story without thanking Sue Fitzgerald, RN, for the ride from the hospital to the airport, and Portia Hein and Phillip Martin, for letting me shack up in their Texas abode to write this story.

On a lighter note, here is a picture of my brother and me wearing paper bags on our heads!

*T*his is actually a picture of a picture, taken long ago, which I have on my office desk. It was snapped at the farmhouse of novelist Vance Bourjaily, one of my teachers at Iowa; I was watching over his place while he and his family were on an extended trip abroad. To my right, holding the black lamb, is my classmate (and still friend) Barbara Grossman. To my left, holding along with me the white lamb, is Jane Howard, who taught at Iowa and who remained a dear friend until her death a couple of years ago. To Jane's left is Steve Mortensen, another student at Iowa. At the far right is my dog Mollie, who lived another twelve years. The lambs were orphaned, and one of my charges was to bottle-feed them four times a day.

I'm half Korean-American; I call myself a Eurasian, but the truth is that I don't know the first thing about my Korean ancestors, although several of my stories have been based on their lives. I was raised a white girl, so I've had to make everything up. I scrape together bits and pieces from things my mother or aunts have told me. I read books by and about Koreans and Korean Americans. I stare a long time at old photographs. This is one photograph that spoke to me. My mother is the little girl in front in the dress. She said she loved that dress because it was decorated with a little cluster of bright red berries. The day after the photograph was taken, her two elder sisters sneaked off in the night with a bunch of family photographs, their belongings, and some linens (my grandparents owned a laundromat), and eloped with their boyfriends. No one saw them again for a couple of years. I rubbed those two sparks together for a while—the berries on the dress and the elopements—and it started one of my stories.

TIM KEPPEL

It is not that we are connoisseurs of chaos, but that we are surrounded by it, and equipped for coexistence with it only by our fictive powers.

When I read this quote by Frank Kermode, I immediately thought of Colombia. Of course, every place has its share of chaos. The trick is to make order out of that chaos, if not art. I had the pieces of this story (along with many more) swirling in my head for some time, waiting for something to coalesce around. Then came the earthquake.

A grad-school friend landed a job in Fargo, North Dakota; I landed one here. How important is a sense of place to our lives? When you live in Colombia, it tends to be a factor. Nabokov said he recognized the challenge of inventing the U.S. since it had taken him so many years to invent Russia.

Isn't that what we do? We constantly invent the place where we live, and our place in that place. No offense to the Fargoians, but I think I'll stay where I am.

DEBRA INNOCENTI

"Acacia" evolved from pieces of stories about my family and hometown, many told by my father. Mine is a family of Italian immigrants who came to Texas along with many others to work the railroads and make their fortunes. When the railroad projects eventually fell through, some became farmers and ranchers.

I grew up in the country, in the southeast part of Texas. The landscape is dry and there is often a tested hardness about the people who sprung from it. In a book that had a great effect on me, *New Ground*, Carl Bredahl writes that significant to Western writing is a response to surface, what has long troubled the human imagination because it is easier to look beyond the land in an attempt for absolutes and ultimate truths. In the stories I love, the land itself is a character with its own will, and has in part formed who its people are and how they communicate.

Acacia is an important symbol to me. It is a short, thorny tree that has mastered survival in a dry, hot terrain, and still manages to bloom surprisingly delicate yellow blossoms.

My great-grandfather, Giocomo Zandonatti
(with mustache), and his two sons, Ben and Angelo.

℘AST CONTRIBUTING AUTHORS AND ARTISTS
Many of issues 1 through 39 are available for eleven dollars each.

Robert A. Abel • Linsey Abrams • Steve Adams • Susan Alenick • Rosemary Altea • Julia Alvarez • A. Manette Ansay • Margaret Atwood • Kevin Bacon • Aida Baker • Russell Banks • Brad Barkley • Kyle Ann Bates • Richard Bausch • Robert Bausch • Charles Baxter • Ann Beattie • Barbara Bechtold • Cathie Beck • Jeff Becker • Janet Belding • Sallie Bingham • Kristen Birchett • Melanie Bishop • James Carlos Blake • Corinne Demas Bliss • Valerie Block • Joan Bohorfoush • Harold Brodkey • Danit Brown • Kurt McGinnis Brown • Paul Brownfield • Judy Budnitz • Christopher Bundy • Evan Burton • Michael Byers • Christine Byl • Gerard Byrne • Jack Cady • Annie Callan • Kevin Canty • Peter Carey • Ron Carlson • Brian Champeau • Mike Chasar • Robert Chibka • Carolyn Chute • George Makana Clark • Dennis Clemmens • Aaron Cohen • Robert Cohen • Evan S. Connell • Ellen Cooney • Rand Richards Cooper • Rita D. Costello • Wendy Counsil • William J. Cyr • Tristan Davies • Toi Derricotte • Janet Desaulniers • Tiziana di Marina • Junot Díaz • Stephen Dixon • Michael Dorris • Siobhan Dowd • Eugenie Doyle • Tiffany Drever • Andre Dubus • Andre Dubus III • Wayne Dyer • Ron Egatz • Barbara Eiswerth • Mary Ellis • Susan Engberg • Lin Enger • James English • Tony Eprile • Louise Erdrich • Zoë Evamy • Nomi Eve • Edward Falco • Lisa Fetchko • Susan Fox • Michael Frank • Pete Fromm • Daniel Gabriel • Ernest Gaines • Tess Gallagher • Louis Gallo • Kent Gardien • Ellen Gilchrist • Mary Gordon • Peter Gordon • Elizabeth Graver • Andrew Sean Greer • Gail Greiner • John Griesemer • Paul Griner • Patricia Hampl • Christian Hansen • Elizabeth Logan Harris • Marina Harris • Erin Hart • Daniel Hayes • David Haynes • Daniel Hecht • Ursula Hegi • Amy Hempel • Andee Hochman • Alice Hoffman • Jack Holland • Noy Holland • Lucy Honig • Ann Hood • Linda Hornbuckle • David Huddle • Siri Hustvedt • Stewart David Ikeda • Lawson Fusao Inada • Elizabeth Inness-Brown • Bruce Jacobson • Andrea Jeyaveeran • Charles Johnson • Leslie Johnson • Wayne Johnson • Thom Jones • Tom Miller Juvik • Cyril Jones-Kellet • Elizabeth Judd • Jiri Kajanë • Hester Kaplan • Wayne Karlin • Andrea King Kelly • Thomas E. Kennedy • Jamaica Kincaid • Lily King • Maina wa Kinyatti • Carolyn Kizer • Carrie Knowles • David Koon • Karen Kovacik • Jake Kreilkamp • Marilyn Krysl • Frances Kuffel • Anatoly Kurchatkin • Victoria Lancelotta • Jennifer Levasseur • Doug Lawson • Don Lee • Peter Lefcourt • Jon Leon • Doris Lessing • Debra Levy • Janice Levy • Christine Liotta • Rosina Lippi-Green • David Long • Nathan Long • Salvatore Diego Lopez • Melissa Lowver • William Luvaas • Richard Lyons • Bruce Machart • Jeff MacNelly • R. Kevin Maler • George Manner • Jana Martin • Lee Martin • Alice Mattison • Jane McCafferty • Judith McClain • Cammie McGovern • Eileen McGuire • Susan McInnis • Gregory McNamee • Jenny Drake McPhee • Frank Michel • Nancy Middleton • Alyce Miller • Katherine Min • Mary McGarry Morris • Mary Morrissy • Bernard Mulligan • Abdelrahman Munif • Manuel Muñoz • Karen Munro • Kent Nelson • Sigrid Nunez • Ron Nyren • Joyce Carol Oates • Tim O'Brien • Vana O'Brien • Mary O'Dell • Chris Offutt • Laura Oliver • Felicia Olivera • Stewart O'Nan • Elizabeth Oness • Karen Outen • Mary Overton • Patricia Page • Ann Pancake • Peter Parsons • Roy Parvin • Karenmary Penn • Susan Perabo • Constance Pierce • Steven Polansky • John Prendergast • Jessica Printz • E. Annie Proulx • Kevin Rabalais • Jonathan Raban • George Rabasa • Margo Rabb • Mark Rader • Paul Rawlins • Nancy Reisman • Linda Reynolds • Anne Rice • Alberto Ríos • Roxana Robinson • Paulette Roeske • Stan Rogal • Frank Ronan • Elizabeth Rosen • Janice Rosenberg • Jane Rosenzweig • Karen Sagstetter • Kiran Kaur Saini • Libby Schmais • Natalie Schoen • Jim Schumock • Lynn Sharon Schwartz • Barbara Scot • Amy Selwyn • Catherine Seto • Bob Shacochis • Evelyn Sharenov • Sally Shivnan • Ami Silber • Al Sim • George Singleton • Floyd Skloot • Roland Sodowsky • Gregory Spatz • Brent Spencer • L.M. Spencer • Lara Stapleton • Barbara Stevens • John Stinson • George Stolz • William Styron • Karen Swenson • Liz Szabla • Paul Theroux • Abigail Thomas • Randolph Thomas • Joyce Thompson • Patrick Tierney • Andrew Toos • Patricia Traxler • Jessica Treadway • Rob Trucks • Kathryn Trueblood • Carol Turner • Christine Turner • Kathleen Tyau • Michael Upchurch • Lee Upton • Gerard Varni • A. J. Verdelle • Daniel Villasenor • Sergio Gabriel Waisman • Daniel Wallace • Ren Wanding • Mary Yukari Waters • Jamie Weisman • Lance Weller • Ed Weyhing • Joan Wickersham • Lex Williford • Gary Wilson • Robin Winick • Terry Wolverton • Monica Wood • Christopher Woods • wormser • Celia Wren • Calvin Wright • Brennen Wysong • Jane Zwinger

*Tante Gretchen and
"Uncle" Joe, L.A., 1948*

Coming soon:

I looked at him as if seeing him there would tell me that
nothing this wrong could possibly be happening. His eyes
held me, his mouth open and words splitting out of him as I
moved toward the winch to hit the shutoff, and saw the cable
pull slowly through his jeans just above his knee.

from "Another Perfect Catastrophe" by Brad Barkley

We're driving through the Lincoln Tunnel en route to
Jersey when Ivan turns off the tape player and puts his hand
on my thigh. I know what that means. It means he's gearing
up to tell me the story. He'll be telling it in a way which
suggests that he has never told me this story before, that he has
never told it to anyone, that it's coming straight to me from his
heart, where he has saved it for me all these years.

*from "Down the Shore Everything's All Right"
by Michelle Richmond*

The few animals stupid enough to be out in these condi-
tions would be, well, just that—*stupid*. And to eat the meat of
any such animal would be risky. It was known that the *stupid*
would roll right out of the meat onto the fork, off the fork
into the mouth, and directly into the character and demeanor
of the consumer. That dictum is as old as hunting itself.

from "Memory of Hard Rain" by Brian Ames